The Sapphire Bride

Central City Brides, Book 2

CYNTHIA WOOLF

Photo credits – Novel Expressions, Period Images,
Deposit Photos, Romcon Custom Covers

ISBN: 1938887913
ISBN- 978-1-938887-91-8

DEDICATION

For Jim. Thank you for being my greatest cheerleader, my husband, my lover and my best friend. You keep me fed, put me to bed when I fall asleep at my desk and take care of me in so many more ways than I've listed here.

I love you, sweetheart!

FOREVER AND A DAY!

ACKNOWLEDGMENTS

For my Just Write partners Michele Callahan, Karen Docter, and Cate Rowan

For my wonderful cover artist, Romcon Custom Covers

For my wonderful editor, Linda Carroll-Bradd, you make my stories so much better. I don't know what I would do without you.

CHAPTER 1

Monday, October 4, 1869, New York City

Bang! Bang! Bang!

The sound of someone pounding on her front door reached Ava Lewis in the kitchen where she was shining a sapphire ring she'd just finished making. She wiped the abrasive cream from her hands onto a towel, rather than on the pristine white apron that covered her favorite lavender dress. By the time she reached the living room and padded across the carpet runner to the front door, her hands were free from the cream. She checked the clock on the fireplace mantle, only six-fifteen in the morning.

Who would be here this time of the morning?

Bang! Bang! Bang!

"I'm coming. Hold your horses."

She opened the door wide.

"What do you want?"

The person standing in the hallway wore

a light colored field jacket wrinkled from long wear and pants, with the knees nearly worn through, had definitely seen better days.

"Jeffrey! Is that you? Come in."

"Hi Sis."

Her twin brother, boasting long sable brown hair and a full beard, stumbled into her living room and fell unconscious to the floor. His carpet bag next to him in the hallway.

"Jeffrey!"

Ava shut the door and knelt by her brother. She checked his pulse and, thank the Lord, found one.

What is he doing here? He's supposed to be in Peru on a dig.

She slapped his face.

"Jeffrey. Jeffrey."

Getting no response she ran to the kitchen, grabbed her smelling salts. She ran back to her brother who lay unmoving on the floor, and placed the smelly bottle under his nose.

He pushed away the foul stench and opened his eyes, blinking several times.

"Thanks, Sis. Sorry about passing out in your doorway. I need a place to stay. I won't

9

lie to you. I've got some bad people after me."

"What do you mean bad people?"

She noticed he kept his left hand pressed to his right side.

"Are you hurt? Let me see. Can you stand? Let's get you to the sofa. Take my hand and I'll help you."

He grasped her hand and stood.

"Where's my bag?"

She helped him over to the sofa where he sat heavily.

"Probably still in the hallway. I'll get it. I wasn't too concerned with luggage when you passed out on my floor."

She opened the door, saw the carpet-bag in the hall and brought it inside, setting it next to the green brocade sofa where he sat.

"Thanks, Sis. I'm hurt pretty badly. I wasn't sure I'd make it here. People are trying to kill me because of what I carry."

He pulled on her arm with his right hand. His grip like iron, then his strength gave out.

"You need to take the bag and run. Leave me here and go as far away as you can."

"Why? What's in the bag?"

"I'll tell you later."

"I don't understand. I can't just leave you."

He grimaced as he held his side and she saw a trickle of blood run down his hand.

"You need to see a doctor. You're bleeding."

She ran to the kitchen and came back with several towels.

"Here, press these to your wounds."

He closed his eyes and grimaced as she pulled his hand away from his side. The wound appeared deep, but, oddly, wasn't bleeding heavily. She placed a folded towel over the injury, pressed and waited until he replaced his hand on the cloth.

"This injury is nothing. Don't you understand? You. Have. To. Run. You must go and go far."

She stood and paced in front of the sofa.

"Even if I were to agree with you, I don't have anywhere to go. I've worked so hard to become a jeweler. The only female one in New York City. I didn't marry because every man I met expected me to give up my jewelry designing. People like to talk to me about my designs but when it comes to purchasing my wares, they balk.

It's too unusual, not traditional enough. For the pieces that do sell, the owner of the store says he created them. I'd love to go somewhere else, but I have nowhere to go."

She stopped moving and cocked her head to the side.

"I...I've been thinking about becoming a mail-order bride, but haven't done it yet."

He smiled and nodded.

"Great. Do it. Go sign up now. Leave as soon as you can. Tomorrow, if you can. I'll tell you everything when you get back."

"Jeffrey, you're scaring me."

Her heart pounded, her stomach turned over as fear worked its way through her body.

You're all I have since Mama and Daddy died when we were fifteen. We raised each other, you more than me. Don't you die on me.

"Good. Be scared. The people after me are dangerous and won't hesitate to kill you."

She jutted her chin toward his side.

"Who's after you? Is that what happened to you? Did the men chasing you do this?"

"Yes. I'll explain everything after you get back from the mail-order bride place. I promise. Please. Go now. My time is short."

Tears formed in her eyes and she tried hard to keep them from falling. "I can't just leave you like this. You need a doctor."

"I can't go to a doctor. Emmett will be looking for that. Besides, there's nothing a doctor can do for me anyway. The antidote is very rare. So go to the bride place. Go. Now, Ava. Please. I'll be here when you get back."

"Antidote? Have you been poisoned? Who is Emmett?"

He closed his eyes and sighed.

"Yes, the blade that cut me was rubbed with the skin of a poison dart frog. It's very rare and the antidote even rarer."

He groaned and slipped a bit more sideways on her sofa.

"All right. I'm going."

Ava washed her hands of any remaining cream, took off her apron, donned her black wool coat and grabbed her reticule. She returned to the living room and saw Jeffrey leaning completely on his side.

"Here this will be more comfortable for you."

She raised his feet and legs so he lay properly on the sofa.

He sighed. "Thank you. That is better."

"Would you like a glass of water before I go?"

"Please. That would be great."

She got him the water and placed the glass on the coffee table in front of him.

"I'll be back as quickly as I can."

"I'll be here, but hurry."

She nodded and headed out the door to Matchmaker & Co.

*****

The office was located in a beautiful three-story brownstone. When the cab arrived, she smiled when she saw the bright blue door at 221 Baker Street. That was about the only thing today that made her smile.

She smoothed away any wrinkles in her skirt with her shaking hands and then walked into the office. Ava's greatest fear was returning home and finding Jeffrey already dead. She had to hurry, hopefully the process was fast.

A lovely woman with fiery red hair and wearing a gorgeous emerald dress sat behind a large oak desk.

She looked up.

"May I help you?"

Ava stepped forward with her trembling hand extended.

She picked the first name that came to her. "Yes, I'm Jane Smith and I want to be a mail-order bride."

Ava felt odd answering to the phony name, but she must get used to it. This is who she was from now on. Jane Smith.

Mrs. Selby held Ava's hand a bit too long.

"I'm sorry you must think me rude, but I've never seen anyone with violet colored eyes before. Anyway," she let go of Ava's hand. "Miss Smith, I'm Margaret Selby. Come sit down and tell me all about yourself and what you're looking for in a groom."

Ava sat in the wooden chair in front of the desk, her spine ramrod straight and not touching the ladder-back.

"I'm looking for a kind man who always holds his temper in check. I need someone who will let me continue to make my jewelry. I work on consignment from home, but my dream is to open my own shop someday."

Mrs. Selby nodded.

"I'm afraid I don't have any candidates who say they want a jeweler for a bride."

Ava ducked her head and frowned a bit.

"No, I, uh don't suppose you do."

"So tell me what else you need besides a kind man with no temper."

She thought about her parent's marriage. *I want what they had. Someone to laugh with and cry with. Who loves children and isn't afraid to show affection.*

"I want someone who wants children and a loving marriage at least in the future, not right away."

"I think I have someone. You don't mind if he owns a saloon, do you?"

Thank God. I'm getting a quick match. That should make Jeffrey happy.

"No, I don't mind as long as he's not overindulging in his liquor. I don't want a drunkard."

Margaret shook her head. She looked at a couple of folders, then moved those out of the way and put another on top of the stack.

"No. None of us want that. This man is named Seamus Madigan. He is Irish. Does that matter?"

Ava shook her head. "Not to me."

"He owns three saloons in Central City in the Colorado Territory. How does that sound so far?"

"Fine. That seems quite far away." She added under her breath, "Jeffrey should be happy with that."

Margaret leaned forward.

"What?"

Ava shook her head.

"Nothing." Ava shifted in her chair. "Did your Mr. Madigan send a letter or a picture?" *Though what he looks like doesn't matter as long as he's far away.*

Margaret opened the file folder, shuffled through the papers until she found what she looked for.

"As it happens, he sent both. In the picture, he's the second from the left. He says he's six feet two inches. The man in the middle must be a giant."

Ava took the picture from Mrs. Selby's extended hand.

"He appears to be very handsome. All of them do. Do you think he'll be interested in a jewelry maker for a wife?"

"I think any man would be lucky to have you as a wife. Here is his letter."

Ava took the proffered letter and began to read.

September 15, 1869

Dear Mrs. Selby,

Your name and address were given to me by Jack and Rita Colton who have successfully used your services.

My name is Seamus Madigan but everyone calls me Lucky. I guess I pretty much live up to my nickname in every aspect of my life except for marriage. I have never found the perfect woman, so I'm turning to the professionals. In this case that is you.

Jack and Rita are very happy with your pick of potential mates. I hope you can do as well for me.

A little background about myself. As you can probably tell from my given name, I'm Irish. I own three saloons which I won in card games. I'm very careful when I play now as I have no intention to lose any of the saloons. They are all money makers.

I would like to find a woman who is not judgmental about what I do for a living. I need a woman who can entertain herself and doesn't expect me to be with her all the time.

Mrs. Selby, I'd be very grateful if you could find me someone right for me.

Sincerely,
Seamus "Lucky" Madigan

Mrs. Selby gazed at Ava with a smile on her face.

"Well, what do you think, Jane? I believe he's just what you are looking for...someone who will let you continue with your jewelry making."

"I believe you're correct in that he's the perfect gentleman for me. When can I leave for Central City and Mr. Madigan?"

Mrs. Selby cocked an eyebrow.

"We can get you tickets for tomorrows train if you like. Is there a particular hurry?"

"Yes, I'd rather not pay another month's rent." Feeling a little nervous, she wondered if this was enough of an excuse.

Ava had thought about this particular question all the way over. What was her hurry? She couldn't very well divulge that her injured brother told her to run, but technically the rent was due, though she had another week before it was late.

"Then I'll get you the tickets and you can pick them up at five o'clock, before I close for the day. You'll have train tickets, but you'll have to buy the stagecoach tickets when you reach Atchison, Kansas. Mr. Madigan has provided money for the tickets and your expenses along the way. The stagecoach will take you to Denver, where you'll have to buy more stagecoach tickets to Golden City and then you'll have to buy another ticket for the wagon to Central City. It's quite the journey. Are you sure you're ready to leave so soon?"

"Oh, yes." *Relief flooded her. The sooner the better.* "Will this man know I'm coming?"

"Yes. While I'm out, I'll send a telegram to let him know that you'll be there on or about the nineteenth or twentieth of October. I understand that the trip is not for the faint of heart."

Ava put her hand to the lace at the neck of her blouse.

"Oh my, that does sound rather daunting, doesn't it? Good thing I'm not some whimpering miss who is frightened by my own shadow."

Mrs. Selby chuckled.

"I believe you and Mr. Lucky Madigan will suit."

"I think so, too. I'll see you in a few hours."

*****

Ava hailed a cab and hurried home,

worried about what she would find there. Her home was the back apartment on the first floor of the four story apartment building. When she arrived, she saw blood on her front door where Jeffrey had knocked. She hadn't noticed the red marks before. She'd been in too much of a hurry.

As she walked in she found her brother asleep on the sofa. When she entered the room, he awoke and sat up.

"Oh, Ava, you startled me."

"I'm glad you were able to get some rest. Will you let me look at your wound now?"

"Only if you tell me you're leaving soon."

"Is tomorrow soon enough?"

"Yes. Today would be better but tomorrow will do."

He closed his eyes and exhaled a long breath, then slumped to the side.

"Jeffrey!"

She shot forward and righted him.

"Ava, I'm not going to make it. The poison will kill me in a few more hours."

"No, Jeffrey. Come with me. We can leave together."

"I can't and I don't want the men after

me to know about you. I would have been here sooner but I had to make sure I wasn't followed. I hope I achieved that."

She sat next to him and swiped the hair out of his eyes.

"Tell me why they are after you."

He jutted his head toward the end of the couch.

"Hand me my bag."

She retrieved the piece of luggage and gave it to him. He was so pale. When she sat next to him again, she wanted to take him in her arms and make it all better, but she couldn't.

From the valise, he pulled out a small leather pouch about the size of a pint jar and handed it to her.

She opened the pouch and her eyes widened. Ava poured some of the contents into her hand, filling her palm with diamonds, sapphires, rubies and emeralds. The gems were hundreds of times more than the stones she had for her jewelry. The jewels had to be worth hundreds of thousands of dollars. She'd never seen so much wealth, so many dazzling jewels all at once in her life.

"Where did you get all of this? From

your excavation in South America?"

He nodded and the small movement seemed to tire him.

"I found an Incan burial tomb in Peru. The men after me seem to think I should give all these to them because I'm not Peruvian. But then, neither are they. They are thugs from New York hired by my rival, Emmett Walsh. I had a deal with the government, which said I could keep half of what I found. This is my half. Emmett had the same agreement but didn't find as much, so he wants mine. Don't let him have them. These are yours now. You own them fair and *legally*. There is a paper with the agreement with the government proving that you own these jewels so you can open your own shop to sell your jewelry designs after you're married and Walsh isn't a threat to you. "

She looked at her twin, and saw the same sable brown hair and violet eyes that she herself had. How could she just stand by and let him die?

Ava saw them playing together, climbing the trees and the sitting on top of the house and eating their lunch, pretending they were on a high mountain and had just planted the American flag.

There had been an old house, shack really, that their parents had lived in while the big house was being built. The house was only about fifteen feet wide and she would use a broom pretending it was a paddle and Jeffrey would use one as well so he had a paddle, too. One of them paddled from the open door, the other through an open window across the room from the door. They were pirates on the river.

She remembered her parent's funeral and Jeffrey telling her he'd take care of her, even though he was only a few minutes older than she was he'd always acted as though it had been years.

And as they got older, they'd stayed as close as Jeffrey's job would let them. Being an archeologist meant he was gone on digs most of the time. That's where he was supposed to be now, instead he lay dying on her sofa.

Ava put the gems back into the pouch and set it on the table in front of the sofa.

"Since you won't see a doctor, you should at least get into my bed. I'll make you some tea. If you're right about the poison and I assume you are, nothing says you can't be comfortable before you…"

Her voice broke and she couldn't help the tears that flowed from her eyes.

"Before you die."

Jeffrey held up his left arm and beckoned her to come cuddle.

"Promise me, Ava. You won't let Walsh have the jewels. Promise me."

"I promise."

"Now, let me hold you for a while, Sis. You need it as much as I do."

She nodded and slid under his arm.

They sat there, holding each other, for more than an hour. Then Ava heard Jeffrey's labored breathing become more so and then the room was quiet. She didn't want to move. Didn't want to see the face of her dear brother as he lay dead on her sofa knowing she would have to leave him and couldn't give him the burial he deserved.

She cried harder and stayed where she was, holding him, wishing things were different and he would wake up, laugh and tell her he'd fooled her again.

But she knew she would never hear his laughter again. Never see his violet eyes sparkling with mischief or have him hold her when some man had broken her heart.

Finally, the time had come to collect the tickets from Mrs. Selby.

Ava laid Jeffrey on the sofa and covered him with the blanket from the back of the couch as though he was sleeping.

She pressed cold wash cloths on her eyes hoping to ease the swelling present from her crying.

*****

When she arrived at Matchmaker & Co. Mrs. Selby gave her the tickets. If she noticed Ava's swollen eyes, she didn't say anything.

"Here is the money Mr. Madigan sent for the tickets. There is two hundred dollars here to cover your expenses. It was also to buy any clothes you might need but there is no time for that, you'll have to buy what you need when you get to Denver."

Ava took the money and put it in her reticule.

"Thank you, Mrs. Selby for everything. I feel so *lucky* to have seen your advertisement when I did."

"I hope you have a good trip and a wonderful life. Drop me a line once in a while and let me know how you are."

"I will. Thank you."

*****

Ava returned home, hoping that somehow, Jeffrey would greet her on her return. But he didn't. He lay just as she'd left him, in quiet repose.

She went to the kitchen, got cleaning supplies and removed the blood from the outside door. She didn't want anyone to know he was here. She hated doing that, hiding him, but she had to cover as much distance as she could before his body was found.

Then she packed both hers and Jeffrey's bags with her belongings. There was no need to take anything but the clothes and, of course her jeweler's tools, the jewelry she'd already made and still had to sell, Jeffrey's bag of gems and food for the journey.

She split Jeffrey's jewels in half and sewed them into two hidden pockets in her skirt. So they wouldn't rattle, she put a sock in the pocket, too. Now they were out of sight. Safe.

Now she was ready for her trip to Central City and a new life.

CHAPTER 2

Atchison, Kansas, October 8, 1869

Ava made sure she'd gotten a seat by the window on the train. She'd never been out of New York except for one time their parents took them to visit her father's great aunt in Connecticut. They'd been five and she hadn't paid much attention to the scenery.

This time, however, she'd loved seeing the change from New York's tall buildings to smaller towns with only a few buildings taller than ten stories to really small towns with only houses and a few businesses like a general store. She wondered what Central City was like. Did it have tall buildings made of concrete? Or was it like the small towns with only one and maybe two story buildings?

At times like this she especially missed Jeffrey. He would have loved that she was finally having an adventure, seeing new sights. She rode through farm land where there was very few houses but lots of fields of what she figured was wheat and some corn and some she didn't even have a guess as to what the field contained.

While she traveled she thought about what she would do with the gems. She wanted to make jewelry with them. Some of the larger stones would have to be cut into smaller stones and all of them would need to be cut to reveal the heart, the beauty of the stone. She'd like to open her own shop but she'd also need to sell in New York, if possible, Denver for sure.

Finally they reached Kansas. She was glad they'd reached Atchison in good time. The train ride left a lot to be desired, but would be considered extremely comfortable compared to the stagecoach. She knew from what she'd read while on the train, that the travel by stagecoach would be very uncomfortable. Often the benches weren't padded but simply planks of wood, either two or three across.

If the coach she rode in had the three benches across seating, she would do her best not to be in the middle row because the seat had no back support. Her back would be hurting in nothing flat. Maybe children would be traveling who could sit in the middle or perhaps if they were lucky, no one would have to sit in the middle.

As luck would have it, her stagecoach only had the two benches across from each other, thank goodness, but they were not padded. She pulled out her coat from the luggage and folded it to sit upon.

They made stops about every ten to twelve miles, to change horses and let the six passengers stretch or use the facilities, such as they were.

Some of the stations were better and bigger than others. Families or perhaps a husband and wife ran the bigger stations. Food was available and, if one desired, one could stay overnight.

Ava declined to stay at any of the stations. She wanted to get to Central City with all haste.

The smaller stations were run by bachelors and didn't offer food. It mattered not what kind of station they stopped at, Ava made sure to get out and walk around.

They reached Denver on the twentieth of October at about ten-thirty in the morning. The stage to Golden City didn't leave until the next morning. She would have to get a room for the night, which at this point in time sounded like heaven. Ava picked up her bags and headed to the hotel across from the stage stop.

"Miss Smith? Miss Smith?"

She realized it was her name the male voice called and looked around for the speaker.

A tall, blond man headed toward her from a buggy on the street at the end of the platform. As he got closer she recognized him from the picture he sent, even though he was not in uniform as he was in the picture.

"Miss Jane Smith?"

Ava looked up into the nicest brown eyes. They were a dark amber color, almost like a tiger's eye stone. He was dressed in a black wool pants, vest and a white shirt with the sleeves rolled up.

"I'm Jane Smith."

He removed his hat.

"I'm Lucky, I mean Seamus Madigan."

She smiled. He was even more handsome in person than he was in his picture.

"I don't mind calling you Lucky. I saw that's the way you signed your letter."

He ran his hand behind his neck.

"I haven't been Seamus since I was a lad. My mother always called me that."

She loved the deep baritone and the Irish lilt to his voice.

"Would you prefer I called you Seamus?"

"No. Lucky is fine. I'm sure to answer you that way."

He smiled and showed straight white teeth. His smile reminded her of one a mischievous imp would have.

"What are you doing here, Lucky? I hadn't expected to see you until I reached Central City."

She put her hand to her throat and took a deep breath.

"I seem to be somewhat breathless and I don't know why."

"That would be the altitude. We're very high here compared to New York and you'll find Central City even worse for breathing until you become acclimated. As to why I came to meet you in Denver, one of my friends told me that you would enjoy the trip and be much more comfortable in the surrey. Also, that way you and I can get to know each other before we get married later today."

"Married? Later…*today*?"

"Yes, I didn't see any point in putting it off. Do you?"

"No, I suppose you're right."

He frowned. "I want a wife Miss Smith. Someone I can come home to, who will give me children and care for those children as well as for me. Do you understand? I want a family as soon as possible. That starts with marriage. Did you not understand that from my letter?"

He picked up her two bags and started walking away from the stage depot.

She followed. Her own reasons for being here necessitated she marry, so why was she balking?

"No, I do understand. Things just seem to be moving faster than I had anticipated. Marriage is the start of our lives together. I have no intention of going back and if I don't have to ride on that stagecoach again, I'll be plumb thrilled."

He chuckled.

"That trip is a bad one. I've taken that stage to Kansas before, and for the trip back, I bought a horse and rig then rode all the way back to Central City. It was much more comfortable."

"If I had known that was an option…oh, who am I kidding? I still would have chosen the stage. Safety in numbers, you know."

"That I do."

They approached a sleek black surrey pulled by two matched grays.

"Those horses are beautiful. They look like they could be twins."

"Good eye. They are. Belong to a friend of mine."

He placed her bags in the back seat and held out his hand.

She placed her hand in his and accepted his help into the carriage.

Then he went around the back of the buggy to the other side and climbed up next to her. He took up the reins and released the brake before snapping the reins on the horses' rear ends.

"So what do you want to know about me, Miss Smith?"

Ava hated lying. They were to be married but she couldn't take the chance.

"I think first we should do away with the Miss Smith and Mr. Madigan. I'm Jane."

He looked over at her.

"And I'm Lucky, in more ways than

one. You are quite pretty, Jane, and your eyes are spectacular. I've never seen violet eyes before."

She looked down and felt the heat rise to points in her cheeks. She never had been very good at accepting compliments and knew she always blushed profusely.

"Thank you. They run in my family. I hope at least one of our children will have them. Speaking of children, how many do you want?"

"I had one brother. I want lots of kids. My brother and I were close once but no more."

They drove west toward the mountains. Ava was mesmerized by the majesty of the purple peaks some of which already had snow on top. Denver was a town like many of the others, wooden buildings from one to about four stories tall and lots of people going to and fro. Horse drawn carts, wagons and cabs. But the vista that one could see from Denver was amazing.

"I had my twin brother to torment me growing up, but I'd give anything to have him back now." She dug her nails into her palms to keep her from crying.

"Did he die recently?"

She looked up at him, wanting him to know Jeffrey through her.

"Yes, just before I started this trip. I haven't even had a chance to mourn him, which would be just fine with him. He never wanted to be mourned, but his life celebrated. He was an archeologist."

Lucky put his hand on her knee.

"I'm very sorry for your loss. Archeology sounds like an interesting occupation."

"He loved it, but the job could also be very dangerous."

"How so?"

She closed her eyes and took a deep breath.

"I'm not ready to talk about it yet. The pain of losing him is too new. Can you understand?"

"Yes, of course. Is that why you became a mail-order bride?"

She cocked her head to the side. "I'm twenty-six years old, Lucky. If I want children, I need to get married now before I'm really too old, even though I'm already called an old maid. How old are you?"

"Thirty-three. I've never been married and like you, I am not getting any younger."

"Why have you never married? You're a very handsome man, I'm sure there were and are lots of women who would love to be married to a successful man such as yourself."

"Let's just say I have my reasons, but why haven't you?"

"I'm a jewelry designer and maker by trade. I spent many hours working on my career. Every man, except you, wanted me to give that up once we were married. You, on the other hand, want someone who can entertain herself."

"That's very true. I have three saloons that require my time."

She nodded.

"I understand. Well, we are agreed on children. We both want them and we want more than one."

"Yes. Agreed."

"Tell me about Lucky Madigan. Why are you *Lucky*?"

He lifted an eyebrow.

"Besides having you for a bride?"

She felt the heat rise to her cheeks and she gazed down at her lap.

"That's very nice of you to say."

"I've always been lucky at cards and

games of chance. They started calling me Lucky in the army because I managed to live when others didn't."

He looked straight ahead, as though admitting something painful.

"I'm very glad that you lived. What did you do in the army?"

"I think that is something we should talk about after we're married."

"Afraid the answer will scare me off? I can guarantee it won't. I'm here to marry you and that is what I intend to do."

"I'm glad to hear it. Are you any good at making jewelry ?"

"I was the only woman at the jewelers where I worked. I designed jewelry they sold on consignment. Actually I am the only woman I know in this business, but I love it. I love making art. The fact that someone can wear it, doesn't make it any the less a piece of art."

"Where did you learn to make jewelry?"

"A friend of the family let me watch him all the time and would help me make pieces for my mother." She stopped and looked out at the vista and yet saw nothing. "When my parents died, he took me under his wing and taught me how so I could make a living. He was a kind man. Jeffrey and I had no other relatives and Mr. and Mrs. Goldberg took us in. They didn't have children of their own and had known us and watched us grow up from the day we were born. He's the one who paid for Jeffrey's education. When we lost them, the pain was as though we were losing our parents all over again."

Lucky put his hand on her knee.

"I'm sorry for your loss."

"Thank you."

*****

They were finally out of Denver, leaving all the people, animals and congestion behind them. Open road extended as far as she could see.

"I thought we were getting married right away."

"I said today. We will when we reach Blackhawk."

"Is that near Central City?"

"Yes, they are only about a mile and a half apart."

She nodded and studied the view around her. The road ran through the center of grassy fields that in spring would probably be full of green grass and wild flowers in all sorts of colors. Varieties she wouldn't recognize being from New York. Now the grass was brown and spring seemed a long time away. Yet with the mountains in the distance and the sun shining bright and warm, the scene was…glorious.

"Is the countryside always so pretty here?"

"This is the beginning of autumn. If you think it's pretty now, wait until you see it in June when everything is in full bloom. No land is more beautiful. And when winter comes and the snow blankets the countryside, the view is equally breathtaking."

Ava sat with her hands clasped in her lap, looking out over the landscape.

"I can't wait to see it. Seeing white snow instead of gray will definitely be a change. I hope you're planning on getting me new winter clothes. With the winters in New York all of my clothes have seen better days."

"You look very nice in your lavender dress."

"You're just saying that because we'll soon be married, but I know better. This is my best dress and my favorite but I can see it's beginning to fray at the cuffs and the elbows are nearly worn through." She touched her cuff.

He cocked an eyebrow and gave her an appraising look.

"Now that you mention those things I see them, and if that is your best dress then we had better go see Alice for another one at least. Several would be better. I don't want my wife in anything but the best. If you love the dress you're wearing, then see if she can get it cleaned and…"

She couldn't get the dress cleaned until she found a place to hide her jewels.

"It's more than a matter of having the garment cleaned. Major repairs are needed. A new dress would be cheaper."

"You know, as long as we're going through Golden City on the way, we'll stop, order you some clothing and see if Alice has anything readymade you might like. How's that sound?"

Her nervousness was easing. Lucky was a generous man, but she still wondered if she was doing the right thing.

"Wonderful. I think. I really hadn't thought you'd want to buy me clothes, especially before the wedding. Who is Alice?"

"Alice is the seamstress I use for my employees dresses. She's very good and does more than just dresses for saloon girls. I want you to be happy and if buying you a few dresses makes you happy then I'll buy the clothing."

Ava smiled, leaned over and kissed Lucky on the cheek.

"Thank you. That is very sweet. Oh, here is the remainder of the money you sent to Mrs. Selby. Between the stagecoach tickets and food along the way, there is just over one hundred dollars left."

Lucky grinned.

"Don't be saying that out loud. You'll ruin my reputation. You can keep the money. You'll need to have funds to make whatever purchases you want and if you need more money, just let me know. "

Ava was happy, more so than she'd been in a while. For a short time she could forget that Jeffrey was dead and evil men may be after her to end her life.

For now I won't think about that. Today is my wedding day.

CHAPTER 3

Two hours after they left Denver they were entering Golden City, which wasn't a city at all. It was a small village compared to Denver and miniscule compared to New York. Still the town seemed to have everything they needed. She saw a mercantile, butcher, baker, hotel and a dry goods store in addition to the dress shop, all along the main street of Washington Avenue. The dry goods store was the largest of the buildings and the only one with two stories.

Lucky pulled up in front of Alice's Fine Fashions, set the brake and jumped down to help Ava.

"Jane," he said to her. "Get what you need for the next few days. We'll come back for a more extensive wardrobe in a couple of weeks."

I feel so odd, answering to a fake name, but I must continue if I want to make sure I'm not found.

"All right, if you're sure."

"I'm sure. I've got you by my side and intend to keep you there."

"Good because that's where I intend to stay…right by your side. "

Unless the men who killed Jeffrey find me and I have to run again.

They walked in together and were greeted by a thin woman with pointed chin and long nose, wearing a plain black dress. Attractive didn't describe her…birdlike did.

"Why Lucky who do we have here? A new girl?"

Do I look like a saloon girl? I guess I definitely do need new clothes.

"No, Alice this is Jane Smith. She is to be my wife."

"Oh, well, congratulations. What do we need here? Let me see you young woman."

She reached over, took Ava's hand and led her into the middle of the room.

"Turn for me."

Alice lifted her arm and made circles with her hand.

Ava turned carefully so the gems would not make the skirt looked weighed down. She didn't need the dressmaker to recognize there was something wrong with her dress.

"Very nice. You'll look beautiful in purple, lavender, Royal blue and I think for something a little different maybe red."

"No. No red," said Lucky. "That's Delilah's color, you know that."

Delilah? Who is she and what connection does she have to Lucky?

"Ah, yes, so I do. Perhaps we shall make pink Jane's color."

Does Lucky think of me like one of his saloon girls?

"I'd prefer purple," said Ava.

"Very well, purple it is."

"Do you have something appropriate already made that we can take with us today?" asked Lucky. "It must be a dress befitting a lady not a saloon girl."

Ava sighed with relief. For a moment she was afraid he'd have her dressed in some low-cut satin gown.

"Of course. I always have something completed. Come with me."

She walked into the back room and gestured toward a rack of clothes.

The shop was much smaller than the modiste Ava used in New York. Of course, that shop had three seamstresses.

Ava made a beeline for the rack and

pulled out a lavender dress. The color was similar to the one she wore but the style was much newer. This one had a sweetheart neckline and buttons down the fitted bodice to the waist. Sleeves had a four-or five-inch cuff with buttons matching the bodice. The skirt was full to accommodate small hoops, but Ava would wear three petticoats instead. That would give her enough fullness that the hem wouldn't need redoing.

Alice measured her, brought her a new corset, bloomers, three petticoats and stockings from the drawers under the counter along one wall.

Ava put on all the new clothes. She'd had her old corset for about five years, it was past time for a new one and this particular design was so pretty and lifted her bosom.

She went into the front room where Lucky sat waiting. Ava was still nervous. What if he hated it.

"Well? What do you think?"

She twirled for him.

He stood, smiled, took her hand in his and kissed the top.

"I think you look beautiful. Is that the one you want to wear today?"

"Yes, please." She felt wonderful having a new dress especially for her wedding day. Ava couldn't keep the grin off her face.

"We'll take it Alice. You can send the others up to the Golden Spike when they are done."

"Certainly," said Alice from the door between the waiting area and the shop. She had a notepad in her hand and was writing down the costs of the items.

"Thank you, Alice," said Ava as she carefully folded her old dress to put in her baggage. "You can burn the rest of my old clothes. They aren't even good enough to give to the poor."

Alice smiled.

"You are most certainly welcome. I'll take care of your old clothes. If I can be of any additional assistance, please let me know. Lucky is one of my best customers."

"So I understand," said Ava. "Lucky told me earlier that we'd be back in a few weeks. Maybe since you have my measurements you might have a dress or two made up for me and send them ahead."

"Of course," Alice flourished a hand in front of her, taking in Ava's figure. "I'll love dressing you. You have a wonderful figure and could probably go without that new corset."

"Thank you but I think I'll wear it regardless."

Lucky put his hand on Ava's back.

"Come, my dear. We have a preacher waiting. Goodbye, Alice. Send me the bill."

Alice waved as they left the shop.

"Will do. Goodbye."

Ava waved over her shoulder as Lucky guided her though the door and back out to the surrey. When they reached the buggy, Ava stuffed her dress into Jeffrey's carpet-bag and then let Lucky help her onto the seat.

When they were both settled, he turned to her, his brow furrowed.

"I don't know why you want to keep the old dress. Is it special to you?"

"Yes. It's the last thing Jeffrey gave me. I'm very sentimental about it." *Please don't ask any more about it. I'm not ready to tell you my secret.*

He shrugged.

"You are keeping a dress that is frayed and worn for sentimental reasons. I clearly don't understand women. Are you hungry? Have you eaten today?"

She relaxed relieved at the change in topic.

"I haven't eaten and I'd love to have a hot meal that doesn't consist of beans and bread with coffee so strong it could melt the cutlery."

Lucky laughed.

"I hadn't thought about it like that. Well, you are in luck. We have a great place right here in Golden City. Mary's Whistle Stop Café."

They drove to the café situated on the west edge of town at the crossroads for Central City and Boulder. The building was one-story clapboard, painted a pale yellow with the name in red lettering arched on both of the picture windows, one on either side of the door. Not very different from the cafes back home in New York City.

Lucky ushered her into the restaurant.

"Hiya Lucky," said a young girl of about sixteen. "Having lunch with us today?"

"Hi Sara. Yes, my fiancée and I are on our way to Blackhawk to get married, but I figured I better feed her first. I don't want her fainting from hunger during the ceremony."

He patted Ava's hand as it rested on the

crook of his elbow.

"Jane Smith, this is Sara Richards. Her mother is my cook in the Red Dolly Saloon."

Ava smelled fresh bread and maybe a roast or some other meat cooking. Her mouth began to water.

She held out her hand.

"Pleased to meet you, Sara."

"Likewise, Miss Smith."

"I'm Jane," said Ava. *This girl is friendlier than the waitresses in some of the cafes I visited back home.*

"Okay. Jane. Would you two like to sit by the windows or away from them?"

"Away, please," said Ava. "I feel like I'm on display when I sit near the windows."

"I know the feeling," said Sara as she showed them to a table on the wall farthest from the kitchen.

Lucky held out the chair for Ava.

"Thank you."

"You're welcome," he replied and then seated himself across from her.

"Here are your menus," said Sara as she passed them each a menu. "Our special today is beef stew served with hot rolls and butter."

"That must be the luscious food I'm smelling," said Ava.

"Thank you, Sara. We'll need a few minutes," said Lucky.

"Sure thing."

She stepped away from the table.

Ava looked down at the sheet of paper before her.

"Do you have any recommendations?"

"Everything is good. My favorite is the fried chicken. I don't know what Mary does but it's the best."

Ava leaned forward and lowered her voice.

"You mean there really is a Mary? I thought that was just used to put the patrons at ease. That's what they do in New York."

"No, there really is a Mary and she does all the cooking."

"Well, I'll take your advice and have the fried chicken."

"The portion is half a chicken and probably too much for you, but we can take what is leftover with us. Trust me, the food won't go to waste."

"Why do they call this the Whistle Stop Café? The train doesn't come to Golden

City."

He raised his eyebrows and said conspiratorially. "Ah, but there are plans for one and the depot is supposed to be right next to Mary's here. She's preparing for the future, but makes a darn good living right now because she's the best place to eat in town."

Sara came and took their orders.

"Tell me, Jane, why are you really keeping your dress? Are you really sentimental over a piece of clothing?"

Why was he questioning her? Would he not allow her to keep the dress? She had to until she found a safer place for her jewels.

"Yes, I really am. Right now everything that Jeffrey gave me is precious. He's gone, Lucky. He was my only sibling and my twin. The bonds between twins are closer than any others."

"All right I won't ask again. I'm simply trying to understand."

Sara returned with their dinners.

Ava took a bite of her chicken and was in heaven. The skin was crispy and the spices were unlike anything she'd ever tasted.

"This is delicious. Do you suppose Mary

would part with the recipe?"

He shook his head.

"I doubt it. If everyone could make her chicken at home why would they come to her restaurant?"

"Good point. She's got some incredible seasoning in her dredging. I might have to try and duplicate it. You could be in for some interesting meals."

"You'll have plenty of people to test your cooking on. We'll live above the Golden Spike Saloon and you'll have to use that kitchen."

She couldn't keep the disappointment out of her tone.

"I see. For some reason I thought we'd be living in a house, but no matter. I'll make do."

Lucky ran his hand behind his neck.

A gesture she noticed he did when he was nervous or uncomfortable about something.

"You're being very nice about this."

"Now isn't the time for this discussion. No doubt we will have one about the living situation down the road, such as when we have children, for now living above the saloon is all right."

About twenty minutes later, Lucky leaned back in his chair and patted his stomach.

"That was a fine meal."

She dabbed her mouth with a napkin and then set her cutlery on her plate.

"I'll agree. Mary is an extraordinary cook. The potatoes were fluffy, the gravy smooth and not over salted, the chicken exquisite. The rolls are almost as good as mine."

Lucky raised his eyebrows and sat up straight.

"You make rolls as good as Mary's?"

"No."

She pressed her lips together.

"But you said—"

"I said Mary's are *almost* as good as mine. The rolls and bread I bake are the best you'll ever have, I guarantee it."

"I can't wait to taste your...baking."

Suddenly Lucky's eyes took on a sparkle of mischief. She knew exactly what he was talking about. She might be a virgin but she was not naïve.

"Lucky. Someone might hear you. Behave."

He chuckled.

"Should I be scandalized that you understand my reference?"

"Certainly not. I'm twenty-six remember with a twin brother who told me everything about...well...everything. He didn't want me taken unaware."

"I'm sorry I won't get to meet this brother of yours. I think I would have liked him."

Her throat tightened at the thought of her dear brother. "I'm sure you would have. Just about everyone liked Jeffrey." *Except the people who killed him.*

"Are you ready to go? The trip will take us another two hours or so to reach the church."

"I'm ready. I'm surprised you booked the church. I expected to be married by a Justice of the Peace."

"Reverend Jenkins is trying to reform my friends and me. He said he would perform the ceremony any time we were ready to marry."

She cocked an eyebrow. "So...are you reformed?"

He grinned.

"Do I look reformed?"

"No, actually you look quite handsome

and somewhat dangerous."

He reached across the table and took her hand.

"I'm not dangerous to you."

His eyes, his whole face took on a serious demeanor.

"Never to you."

You're wrong. I could lose my heart to you. You're kind, handsome and will be my husband in less than three hours. Oh yes, you are very dangerous to me.

She thought about her skirt where the jewels from Jeffrey lay and the promise she made to him. They were her backup. Should something go wrong with her marriage, they were what she would live on.

Lucky paid the bill, picked up the leftover chicken Sara had wrapped for them in waxed paper, and then they walked out of the restaurant. When they reached the buggy, Lucky put the food in the back and helped Ava into the front seat.

Once they were back on the road, headed into the glorious mountains, Ava broke the silence.

"So are you ready to tell me more about yourself? How about your friends? Tell me about them."

"Well, there's Jack and Rita Colton. They just got married. Matter-of-fact Jack's marriage to Rita is what convinced me to send for my own bride. You."

Rita turned toward Lucky.

"I can't wait to meet them. I hope Rita and I can be friends since we have some things in common."

I miss my friends. I didn't even get to say goodbye and I can't write them to let them know what has happened to me. Winnie and Emiline will be beside themselves especially when they hear about Jeffrey's body being found in my apartment.

He furrowed his eyebrows.

"What do you have in common? She used to be a dancer."

She ticked the similarities off with her fingers.

"We're both from New York City, we both are mail-order brides and we are both artisans. She was a dancer and I'm a jewelry designer."

He raised his eyebrows in surprise.

"I guess you have more in common than I thought."

"Who are your other friends? Are they married?"

"No neither has married. Robert Wallace is a gunsmith and owns the local gun shop in Central City. Henry Jacobs is the blacksmith."

"Henry must be the big man in the picture."

"He is but why would you think so?"

"Because he's the blacksmith and they are usually very strong."

"Makes sense, I guess. Yeah, Henry is a big one. He's six feet, six inches of solid muscle."

"Sounds like someone to stay clear of."

"Nah, he's a big pussy cat with a heart of gold."

"Why aren't they married yet?"

"I'm sure they will be, just as soon as Matchmaker & Co. finds their brides. There are not a lot of women in Central City or Blackhawk. Most of the women here are saloon girls or prostitutes."

He pointed to the buildings ahead of them.

"Ah, here we are. Blackhawk coming up."

Up the hill and spreading even higher was a small town. The first building was a little white church with wooden stairs from the road to the building sitting on the side of the hill.

She pointed at the structure.

"Is that the church we are going to?"

"Yes. That is Reverend Jenkins church."

He pulled up beside the empty hitching rail and set the brake. Then he came around for Ava.

When she was on the ground he grabbed her hand and walked up the steps. Ava was winded when they reached the top of the fourteen steps.

"I can't believe I'm out of breath from running up just a few stairs."

"It's the altitude, I told you about. You'll get used to the thin air, but the time to get totally acclimated is usually a couple of weeks. In the mean time we'll have to make sure you drink lots of water and take willow bark tea for any headache you may get."

"I thought it was just my nerves."

He smiled.

"Are you nervous?"

"Yes, a little. A woman doesn't get married every day."

"No, I suppose not. Are you ready to go in and get this done?"

She nodded. If she'd been wanting romantic words, she wasn't getting them. Lucky seemed to be treating this like any other business deal and she supposed he was right. This marriage was a business deal and each of them had expectations and brought something to the bargain.

"Yes. Are you?"

"Yes, ma'am. I'm as ready as I'll ever be."

"Then let's get married."

The inside of the church was bright. Light came from the large windows on both the long sides of the building. They faced the altar as they entered and she counted five rows of pews with aisles down the middle and along the walls.

Walking down from the pulpit was a tall, slender man with thinning and graying brown hair.

"Ah, Mr. Madigan. I wondered if that was you coming up the stairs. Glad you decided to join us. Is this your lovely fiancée?"

Lucky took his hat into one hand and extended the other to the reverend.

"Hi, Reverend Jenkins. This is Jane Smith. She has had the good taste to decide to marry me."

"Wonderful. You young people come up here. Excuse me for a minute while I get your witnesses. The reverend went to the back of the building and out the door where he stood on the porch and yelled at the little house next to the church.

He returned in a few minutes with a cheerful-looking woman and tall, strapping young man, who clearly was his father's son, in tow.

"Everyone let me make quick introductions. My wife, Edna, and my youngest son, Toby. This is Miss Jane Smith and you both know Lucky Madigan."

"I'll be Seamus for the record today, Reverend."

"Of course. We don't want any of this to be illegal now do we?"

"No sir," replied Lucky.

Ava looked up at Lucky and smiled.

Today I'm Jane Smith and I will be that for as long as I live if I have to be. Someday, when I'm sure that I'm safe, I'll tell Lucky. Hopefully by that time, he'll love me enough to forgive me. Or better yet, to marry me again as Ava Lewis.

CHAPTER 4

"Do you Seamus James Madigan, take this woman to be your lawfully wedded wife to have and to hold, in sickness and in health, for richer, for poorer, and keeping yourself only unto her, from this day forward?"

The reverend's deep voice practically bounced off the church walls.

"I do."

Lucky's words were almost as loud as the reverends and more certain than ever. He was strong and sure when he said his vows.

Now it was her turn and her mouth was suddenly so dry she wondered if the words would come out at all.

"Do you Jane Ava Smith, take this man to be your lawfully wedded husband, to have and to hold, in sickness and in health, for richer, for poorer, and keeping yourself only unto him, for as long as you both shall live?"

"I do."

She was proud of herself. Her voice was

strong, and she didn't sound like a little girl, but a woman fully grown. She hoped that by including her given name as her middle name the ceremony might be more legal.

"Lucky, do you have a ring?"

"Yes, sir."

The reverend jutted his chin toward Ava.

"Lucky, repeat after me. With this ring I thee wed."

"With this ring I thee wed."

He slipped the ring on Ava's finger.

It was wide and etched on the inside. She would read it later.

"You may kiss the bride," said the reverend.

"Oh yes," said Lucky, then he smiled. "Definitely mustn't miss that."

Cradling her face between his palms he met her lips with his. He touched her lips softly and then harder, sipping at her lips and when she would have pulled back he kept his mouth over hers while his tongue pressed along the seam of her lips, seeming to beg for entrance.

She opened her mouth, just a little and his tongue entered and he deepened the kiss.

Her pulse raced as her eyes widened and she gasped. She'd never been kissed like that before in her life.

When he pulled back he caressed her cheeks with his thumbs.

"Very nice, Mrs. Madigan."

"I really am married. Thank you, husband. My gosh that sounds foreign."

"We'll both have to get used to our new roles, wife."

He chuckled, reached in his pants pocket and pulled out a double eagle coin.

"Will that do, Reverend?"

The reverend smiled and nodded.

"More than do, Lucky, but I'll take the extra for the poor in our community."

"Whatever you want, you've made me a happy man today."

"Good," said the reverend. "I wish you both many long and contented years."

"Thank you, reverend," said Ava.

I hope you are right and the only way that will happen is if Jeffrey's killers don't find me.

"Do you need to discuss anything before you leave, my dear?" asked Mrs. Jenkins.

For a moment Ava was baffled by the question, and then the answer hit her like a thunder bolt.

"Oh, no ma'am. Thank you. I'm well

aware of *all* aspects of marriage."

"Very good," said Mrs. Jenkins.

She was clearly relieved at not having to give a new bride 'the talk'.

Lucky put his arm around Ava's waist and pulled her close.

"Don't worry, Edna. Whatever she doesn't know I'll teach her. We'll learn together."

Edna nodded and smiled.

"You do that, Lucky. A marriage takes working together. The union can't survive, otherwise."

"Yes, ma'am. Wise words that I'm sure we both will take to heart."

He gave Ava a little squeeze.

Ava blinked. She felt his heat from being pressed against his hard body…and she liked it.

"Yes, we will."

"Good. Well you children have a happy life. I hope we'll see you on Sunday," added Reverend Jenkins.

Lucky stiffened.

"Jane can come if she likes, but as for me, you and I have already had this discussion."

The reverend closed his eyes for a

moment.

"I know, but I must always ask."

"And my answer hasn't changed, nor will it, without some sort of miracle."

"Then, I shall pray for a miracle," replied Reverend Jenkins.

Lucky smiled.

"You do that, Reverend. Come on, Jane," he headed toward the door. "We should go. I want to show you your new home."

"Thank you, Reverend," said Ava. *Lucky obviously has something against the church. Perhaps it is simply that the church doesn't approve of his line of work, but then it doesn't approve of me and what I do either, so I cannot blame Lucky.*

Lucky grabbed her hand and they walked out of the church.

Instead of helping her into the buggy, as usual, he wrapped his arms around her waist and kissed her long and hard.

Her arms found their way around his neck and when he pulled back her eyes popped open and she felt lightheaded whether from the kiss or the altitude, she wasn't sure. She chose the kiss because she'd never had a kiss like that.

He was grinning.

"I do like kissing you."

"And I you. The experience is very pleasant."

"You'd never been kissed before?"

"No, our wedding kiss was my first."

"Well, I'll be. I never expected to get a virgin."

Embarrassed by this discussion, she knew she blushed.

"Well you have. May we go now?"

He smiled.

"Yes, we most certainly can."

He took her by the waist and lifted her onto the buggy.

"Oh."

She swallowed hard as he set her on the seat.

"That was very interesting. I felt like I was a butterfly, flying through the air."

Lucky laughed.

"Flying is what I wish we could do now, for the minutes until I have you in my arms will seem like an eternity."

She gasped and put her hand to her throat.

"Lucky, I didn't know you were a poet."

"Neither did I."

He went around the back of the surrey and climbed in. Once the horses were back on the road he slapped their behinds until they were running.

Ava held on to the strap on the canopy brace and looked askance at her husband as they flew along the road.

She shouted over the din of the horses hooves hitting the ground.

"Are we in some sort of hurry?"

"Yes, ma'am we are. I can't wait to have you naked in my arms."

"Oh. My." *The marriage bed. Lucky is in such a hurry and I know there will be pain. Jeffrey told me, but knowing doesn't take away my fear.*

"Oh, yes."

She knew that she and her brother should never have discussed such matters, but they only had each other after their parents died in the house fire that had left her and Jeffrey alone at the age of fifteen. After that, they'd looked out for each other and Jeffrey had taken on the role of parent, even though they were the same age.

The Goldberg's took them in and treated them as their own children, but it wasn't the same. Mrs. Goldberg died when she and

Jeffrey were seventeen and he took on the completion of Ava's education. He told her what he knew about marriage and the marriage bed. But that knowledge didn't help her here.

Before she knew the time had passed they were pulling up in front of a large, two-story brown building. On a huge sign attached to the roof's edge were the words Golden Spike Saloon.

"Home sweet home, my dear."

She released the strap she'd been holding.

"I forgot you live above a saloon."

"Yes, ma'am. Jane, I will build us a house, but for now this is where we live. Shall we go in?"

"I…um…yes, of course. Can you just leave the horse and buggy here?"

"I'll send one of the boys out to take care of the horses and then we'll return it to Jack a little later."

She swallowed hard and looked over at the sign again.

"Shouldn't we return them now?"

Lucky took her hand.

"I know you're frightened of what is to come, but I will do my best to ease you and not hurt you."

"But you will." She felt the heat in her cheeks and ducked her head. "Jeffrey told me."

"I'm still a little uncomfortable that you and your brother discussed this part of marriage, but did he at least tell you there is pleasure to be had as well?"

Ava turned the ring on her finger. Proof of her marriage and the fact that Lucky can do what he wants with her.

"No, he didn't. You must understand, we discussed everything...and I wouldn't have our relationship any other way. I expect you and me to have a much similar relationship. Though I realize that everyone has secrets."

"Not you. What could you have to be secret about?"

She was worried if she told Lucky about the gems, he would be upset that she may have people with murderous intentions after her. But she couldn't tell him. Not yet.

Ava sat up straight. "That's my business and when the situation is such that my secrets are your business then I'll tell you. Just as I hope you'll feel comfortable telling me yours...when the time is right."

He was quiet for a moment and then nodded.

"As you wish...for now. Come, let's go inside."

He went around to her side and held both arms up toward her.

She leaned down and placed her hands on his shoulders. He took her by the waist and swung her around until her feet were on the ground.

Ava giggled. She couldn't help it.

Lucky handed her the chicken from the back, grabbed her bags and headed inside.

She stopped and looked up at the building that would be her new home. She saw the sign with Golden Spike in large red letters nailed to the second floor railing. Music spilled out the doors when they opened to let someone in or out.

Ava heard laughter and talking and yells. There was a woman singing and she had a very nice voice.

Lucky stopped before the door and looked back at her.

"Come on, Jane. Come in to your new home."

They entered and all the sounds she'd heard on the outside were ten or twenty times louder. She didn't know how anyone heard anything.

Lucky headed directly for the stairs. They'd only gone up a couple of steps when the music stopped and the room got quiet.

"Who's the lady, Lucky?" asked the bartender.

Lucky set down the luggage and put his arm around Ava's waist before turning to face the room.

"Ladies and gentlemen, this good woman is my wife, Jane Madigan. I hope you'll treat her with the utmost respect, because if you don't, you'll answer to me."

"Hi, Mrs. Madigan," came the voices from the crowd.

Overwhelmed by all the attention, she blushed, knowing what was coming and afraid that everyone else in the room did, too. She gave them a little wave.

"Hi, everyone. I'm glad to meet you all."

The music started again and the men went back to their drinks and their games of chance, while the women went back to serving and enticing the men to buy those drinks.

Ava looked over the room searching for a woman in red. Delilah. Was she someone special to Lucky?

Lucky picked up the bags and continued up the stairs with Ava following.

When they reached his rooms, he set down the bags, unlocked and opened the door before sweeping her into his arms over the threshold, into the room.

"Lucky!" Shocked she grabbed for his neck to hold on.

He laughed.

"This is threshold to my home. Our home. Every bride deserves to be carried into her new home."

"That's sweet, but you can put me down now."

"I don't think so."

He kicked the door shut and carried her through a room that served as office and parlor. A massive desk took up most of the space in the middle. Before that, he passed a nice sofa done in brown and gold brocade. Not sedate with the gold running through it, but not garish either. On the floor in front of the couch was an oriental rug also in brown with gold designs.

When they arrived at the door across the room from the entrance, he entered shutting the door behind him leaving only the late afternoon light coming from the two windows. This was a corner room with the windows on perpendicular walls to each other.

She was trying very hard to note the things around her and keep her mind off what was coming.

He carried her to his bed and let her slide down his body before she settled her feet on the floor. She was now well aware how much he wanted her.

"Don't you want to wait—"

His lips crashed down upon hers. In answer to the unasked question...waiting was not an option.

"I want you, Jane. Now. You're my wife on paper and I want to make you my wife in truth."

She ducked her head and stared at the floor. Anywhere was safe as long as she didn't look at him. She knew when she saw the need in his eyes she'd be able to deny him nothing.

"I want that, too, but that doesn't mean I'm not still afraid."

Lucky caressed her cheek with his knuckle and spoke softly.

"You have such soft skin."

"I use cream."

He nuzzled her neck.

"Rose cream. I can smell the delicate scent."

Ava could barely breathe, his touch ignited a spark in her and the fire heated her core.

"Yes…rose."

He leaned down caressed her lips with his, while slowly, meticulously unbuttoning her bodice, then her corset and last, he pulled the ribbon on her chemise until it slipped free baring her to his gaze.

Lucky worked his way down her neck.

His kisses, nips and laving of the nips, left trails of fire running through her and all seemed to be heading to her woman's center.

She couldn't believe she was standing in a man's arms, naked to the waist, her body hot with embarrassment, and yet she yearned for more.

"You are so beautiful. I never thought, I'd be so lucky."

Need left her breathless.

"I thought you were always lucky."

"Not with women, just cards."

"Luck can change. Mine has. You think

I'm beautiful." She thrilled at the compliment and want to lock the words away in her heart.

"You are and you have the most amazing eyes. I hope our children have your eyes."

Her body ached and she was on fire from his kisses and touch.

"No children will be coming if we don't get on with this."

He chuckled.

"In a hurry, now, are we? Don't be. We have all the time in the world."

No sooner had he said those words than pounding sounded from the door in the other room.

"Lucky! You bastard! Come face me!"

The woman sounded angry.

Lucky sighed.

"I'd hoped she wouldn't be around today."

He looked at Ava, pointed at her and then at the floor.

"Stay right where you are. Don't move. I'll be right back."

Ava sat on the bed, her anxiety quickly returning with every moment Lucky was gone. She tied her chemise, hooked her corset and buttoned her bodice, and then she stood behind the door and peeked into the other room.

"What do you mean you're married?" the woman screeched.

If she weren't so angry, she would have been a beautiful woman. Her black hair and pale skin were striking. Right now though, anger mottled her complexion and sent her eyebrows into evil-looking slants over dark eyes.

"I told you. I'm married now. We won't be seeing each other anymore."

"So what am I?"

"You're the singer in my saloon. Just as you've always been. We were a nice diversion for each other, Delilah. Let's leave it at that."

She stood with her hand on one hip and pointed at him with the other.

"Diversion. That's what you call what we had together? A diversion?"

"Yes. I told you in the beginning not to fall for me. I wouldn't marry you."

Ava couldn't believe what she was hearing. Did Lucky just finish with this woman last night?

Delilah Monroe flailed her hand in the

air and then pointed at herself.

"I thought that meant you wouldn't marry anyone, not just me."

"I married a woman I can have children with and was lucky enough to find one who hasn't been with anyone but me."

The woman's eyes narrowed and her eyebrows were slashed over them.

"A virgin. You married a goddamn virgin?"

Lucky pointed at the door to leave.

"Yes. Keep your voice down and get out."

Ava had heard enough. She pulled open the door. Anger filled her. She narrowed her eyes and pulled back her shoulders.

"Yes, why don't you leave, Delilah? Lucky is *my* husband now and I don't share."

The angry woman pushed past Lucky and marched over to Ava.

"You bitch."

She raised her hand and slapped Ava across the face.

"I don't know what you did, but you'll regret marrying Lucky. I'll make you very sorry."

"Delilah!" Lucky shouted as he grabbed

the woman by the arms.

Ava sorely wanted to hit her back, but she wouldn't have just slapped Delilah. A solid uppercut to the jaw would be the best. Jeffrey said it was her finest punch. But she didn't do it. With Lucky holding her opponent it wouldn't be ladylike and she didn't want her brand new husband to think she was nothing more than a street brawler.

She glared at Delilah and rubbed the side of her face.

"Get her out of here, before I forget I'm a lady," Ava said to Lucky.

Lucky hauled her toward the door, scowling at the woman.

"Let's go, Delilah. You can take this as notice that you're fired. No one abuses my wife."

"Fired. You can't fire me. I quit."

The woman freed herself from his grip, turned and stalked out of the room.

Lucky closed and locked the door. He leaned against it and then pushed off toward Ava.

"Now where were we?"

Ava shook her head and waved her index finger.

"If you think we are making love after

that scene, you're sadly mistaken. I suggest we take back the buggy to Jack and Rita so you can introduce me to your friends. Maybe by the time we get back here, my anger will have passed."

Lucky smiled.

"You're a feisty little thing aren't you? Okay, let's take back the buggy and you can meet Jack and Rita."

"Good. Do you always lock your door when you're gone?"

He frowned.

"Of course. I don't want people in my rooms. Our rooms. They are our home. No reason exists for anyone to be in here if one of us is not with them."

"Good."

I don't want to have to explain about the gemstones. Not yet anyway.

"Let's go then. Don't forget your jacket. Even though the weather has been mild for this time of year, the temperature is colder up here in the mountains than in Denver and the sun goes down quicker. At least it seems that way because of the mountains. You'll definitely need your coat when we walk back."

He retrieved her wool coat from the sofa

and he held it for her to put on.

"I'm ready."

He opened the door for her then closed and locked it after them. Then he held out his arm for her to take.

She looked up at him and placed her hand through the crook of his elbow, her movements somewhat stilted because of her anger. They walked down the wooden deck to the stairs.

From the top of the stairs almost the entire first floor was visible. Lucky could keep an eye on things without ever going down.

As they descended, she saw Delilah talking to another one of the girls.

Delilah pointed up toward Lucky's rooms then saw Ava and Lucky descending. She stopped talking and leaned back against the bar and glared at Ava.

"I don't like her Lucky." A shiver ran through Ava as she remembered the woman's threat. "Is she really leaving?"

"If she knows what's good for her, she will be gone by the time we return."

"I hope she leaves Central City."

"I can't force her to leave the city, just my saloons. I'm sorry."

He patted her hand where it rested on his arm.

"Never mind. I'm being silly. Let's go meet your friends."

I can't believe she will just let this go. She wanted to marry Lucky and now I believe she has plans for me...plans I won't like.

CHAPTER 5

Lucky and Ava walked out the back door through the kitchen of the Golden Spike Saloon.

As they walked through, Ava saw that the kitchen was not used much, as there were no pots on the stove, just a coffee pot. But the room had great potential. She'd mention the situation to Lucky when they were on better terms and she wasn't so angry with him and with that woman, Delilah. Then again, now was the best time to talk to him. He didn't argue with Ava about the change in plans so she thought he might be in an accommodating mood. After all Delilah had hit Ava. Her face still stung. Redecorating the kitchen was the least he could do to accommodate Ava.

"Lucky, does anyone use the kitchen now? Do you serve meals or food of any kind?"

"Except for a pot of coffee the answer is no, to both of your questions."

"I didn't think so. The kitchen is in terrible shape. I think I can get the stove looking good again, but you need an icebox and those counters need to be replaced. I suggest we eat out until those things are done and then I can cook our meals."

He lifted his eyebrows and nodded.

"We'll talk more about it later. We have places to go and people to see."

They took the buggy through town. She would call it picturesque if there weren't so many people. A constant stream of people walked the boardwalks and entered or exited the stores. Most of the buildings were one-story and made of wood only. A few like the general store had cemented rocks about halfway up the first floor and then wood from there on up. About every third building was a saloon, gaming establishment or whorehouse. Some were all three.

"Lucky, your businesses are just saloons aren't they?" She ducked her head. "You don't   …um…have…um…prostitutes working for you, do you?"

"No, I don't have any prostitutes in any of my saloons. Just poker and roulette."

She relaxed, pleased by his answer, and let out a breath she'd been holding.

"Roulette? What is that? Is that the game with the wheel?"

Lucky laughed.

"Yes. That's the game with the wheel. I'll take you down and show you how to play if you like."

She smiled and clasped her hands in her lap.

"Yes, I'd like that very much."

Lucky turned onto a long driveway leading to a magnificent house made of red brick.

As soon as they stopped, a young man came out and took charge of the horses.

"Thank you, Barney. Give them extra oats. They put in some hard work today."

"Sure thing, Lucky."

Barney climbed into the buggy and drove away.

"Let's go in shall we?"

"I'm ready."

They walked on a path paved with red flagstone and up two steps to a wide covered porch, supported by four marble pillars. They stood in front of a massive mahogany door that sported a gargoyle for a knocker.

Ava had been in a few homes like this when her parents were still alive. They'd go for Christmas parties and the like, to her father's clients homes.

Lucky lifted the knocker three times. Shortly the door was opened by a matronly woman with kind eyes and silver hair.

Lucky removed his hat.

"Good afternoon Mrs. Bates, are they home?"

She stepped back to let them enter.

"Yes, Mr. Madigan, they're in the parlor."

Lucky grasped Ava's hand in his.

"Come on."

They walked a short way down a hall carpeted with oriental rugs. They muffled their footsteps and were beautiful at the same time. At the first door on the left they stopped.

Lucky knocked on the open door to the parlor.

The man looked up from his paper.

The woman apparently dropped a stitch in her knitting and cursed under her breath.

"Why Lucky, to what do we owe the pleasure? Who is that with you?" asked the woman.

"Rita, Jack, this is Jane Madigan, my wife. We got married today."

"Oh, how wonderful. Sit. Sit. Jane, come sit by me on the sofa," said Rita.

Jack was almost as handsome as Lucky, but he had black hair and arresting dark blue eyes. He'd stood when they entered and she saw that he was a couple of inches shorter than Lucky.

Ava did as Rita asked and sat beside her. She was a pretty woman with curly red hair and emerald green eyes.

Rita's eyes sparkled and she smiled.

"How is New York? Any new changes and Margaret Selby, how is she? The woman saved me."

Ava tilted her head. Though she didn't know it, Margaret had saved Ava's life, too.

"She saved you?"

"Yes, it's a long story, suffice it to say, if she hadn't sent me to Jack, I'd probably be dead."

Ava gasped and put her hand to her throat.

"Oh, my goodness."

"Yes, indeed. Jack and his friends took care of me."

I wonder if I could trust them to take care of me? I'm not willing to risk that right now. For now, I won't say anything. Stick to the plan, Ava. Wait until you're sure you're safe, then talk to Lucky about opening a shop and tell him about the gems. Stick to the plan. Wait until you're safe.

"You're just in time for supper. Please say you'll stay," said Rita pressing a hand to Ava's arm.

"I don't know," said Lucky while he gazed longingly at the door. "We've got—"

"No plans," said Ava with a wide smile. "We'd love to stay."

Supper was delicious and very pleasant. Mrs. Bates, the housekeeper, and Mrs. Potts, the cook, both joined in.

"So," said Jack, with an eyebrow lifted. "You two had your plans for today go awry."

"Yes, we did," said Lucky. "But they were only postponed until tonight. Isn't that right, Jane?"

"I don't know," replied Ava. "I guess it depends on if that Delilah woman is still there when we go back to the saloon."

Ava placed her napkin on the table.

"You two have been very kind to have us to dinner but I believe we have over stayed our welcome. Are you ready to go?"

Her gaze met Lucky's.

He smiled.

"I'm more than ready to get you home."

Ava rolled her eyes.

"Then you should lead the way."

She turned to Jack and Rita.

"Thank you so much. When we get a real home, I shall return the favor."

Lucky grabbed her hand and led her from the room.

"Yes," he said over his shoulder. "Great food, nice talk. See you tomorrow."

As she was being pulled out of the house, she heard Jack and Rita laughing.

"Well, I'm glad we could provide your friends with some entertainment."

He put her hand into the crook of his elbow and she was practically running to keep up.

"Lucky, slow down."

"Nope."

He looked down at her with a smile.

"I got married this afternoon, and I mean to have a wedding night as soon as we get home."

She gazed up at him. "Surely this isn't the first time you've made love with a woman."

As much as I'd rather not think about

him having been with other women, but with Delilah here in town, how can I not.

"Why are you in such a hurry?" She had to admit his ardor made her anxious again. *What if he's in so much of a hurry that he forgets to prepare me?*

He put his hand over hers where it rested on his arm and smiled down at her.

"It's the first time I'll be making love to my wife. The only woman I'll ever have relations with again. Excuse me for being anxious and excited. Aren't you? Excited, I mean."

"Not really. More apprehensive. This is still my first time, remember."

He slowed his pace.

"I remember. Are you still angry about Delilah?"

"Not now. I may change my mind, later. It's a woman's prerogative to change her mind, you know."

The sun had gone down and the sky glowed pink and orange. It was a beautiful view. Lucky had been right about the temperature falling. She was very glad she'd brought her coat.

"No. I didn't know, but now I do and I do my darnedest to keep you happy. That's all I can promise."

They were walking back to the saloon, which, whether she wanted it or not, was her home for now.

"I'm not asking for more than that. I just want to be safe."

"Safe? That's an odd thing to want from a marriage."

"Not really." *Think fast Ava.* "Um…being safe means having all the things a person needs to survive. Food, water, shelter, clothing and you are giving me all those things. Now I just need somewhere to work on my jewelry. A room would do, but the door must have a good lock. I work with gold, silver and gemstones and I can't be packing up everything at night and bringing it home. Sometimes I need to let things sit out and know they are safe."

"I'll set up one of the other rooms upstairs for you."

"What are the rooms used for now?"

"They are used for storage mostly. A couple of the girls live here."

"What *were* they used for?"

He cocked his head.

"What do you think?"

"Prostitution."

"Exactly. When I took over the saloons, I stopped that. I hired the girls who wanted to stay on strictly as servers. They are not allowed to have men in their rooms."

He stood straighter as they walked.

"If they want to make a living on their back, they'll have to do so someplace else."

"Good. I'm glad you don't still have that business. Maybe I can work in one of the rooms next to ours. I would like to keep two rooms next to ours empty. No girls living in them. I'll use the one that attaches to our room and the one next to it will remain empty as a buffer. At least it will give us the semblance of privacy."

"I understand and agree. One of them was occupied by Delilah. She should be gone by now."

"I hope so."

He sighed.

"So do I."

The reached the Golden Spike and went inside.

Lucky looked all around for Delilah.

"I don't see her."

"Me either."

"I'll check with Pete and make sure she's actually gone."

He left her at the bottom of the stairs. She could smell the alcohol in the air. Beer mostly, probably because it was spilled more often than whiskey. The noise from men talking, the piano playing and women dancing on stage was horrendous.

Lucky walked over to the bar, spoke to Pete, the bartender, and returned, smiling.

"Pete must have said she left because you are smiling like the cat that got the cream."

He came close and whispered in her ear.

"I'm smiling because now my sweet little wife can make all the noise she wants to make when we have relations."

She pulled back and looked at him.

"I prefer to think of it as making love. Even though we are not in love now, I hope someday we will be."

"I wouldn't count on it. I promised myself I would never fall in love again. I've seen what love, real or perceived, can do to a man. No, thank you. I don't want that."

What kind of marriage can we have if there is never to be any love? I'd always hoped, believed, we would eventually love each other.

"What have you seen that is so bad?"

He opened the door to their apartment.

"A man who thinks he's in love, does all sorts of silly and stupid things, like bringing her presents, even when they can't afford it. Grinning for no apparent reason. Putting his life on the line to protect hers by joining the army only to find out that she's left you for your brother who stayed home."

She moved through the door into the apartment.

"Ah, I think we hit the nail on the head."

"What?"

He closed the door and locked it behind them.

Ava tossed her coat on the sofa and walked across the room toward the bedroom, unbuttoning her cuffs as she moved.

"You went to fight in the war and your brother stayed home. Your girl got tired of waiting for you and married your brother."

He frowned and added his coat on top of hers on the sofa.

"So, what of it?"

She stopped and looked up at him.

"You were hurt and don't ever want to feel that way again, so you vow never to love another woman."

"That's right. So you understand I won't fall in love with you and I advise you not to fall in love with me. I don't want to hurt you."

"We know where the other stands and that is good."

Ava lowered her gaze for a moment and began to unbutton her bodice, slowly, one button at a time.

He grinned and looked positively predatory.

"Are you teasing me, my little virgin wife?"

"Teasing you?" Her movements stop. "No. I'm trying to slow you down."

"And put off the inevitable? I am making you my wife tonight, but slow is just fine. I'm not answering the door for anyone. I don't care how hard they pound."

As if to emphasize the words, he closed and locked the bedroom door, too.

"Now, where were we?"

He approached her, pulling his shirt over his head rather than deal with the buttons. His chest was covered with a dusting of blond hair and muscles that rippled when he moved. The sight made her core heat.

Then he toed off his boots.

Ava let her dress drop to the floor, followed by her corset. She stood in front of her husband in only her chemise, bloomers and stockings.

Now down to his pants and socks, Lucky dropped his pants and under drawers in one movement, standing before her totally naked except for his socks. And he was ready for her.

Goose bumps covered her arms. She hadn't known what to expect. The paintings at the museum of naked men had not prepared her for someone like Lucky.

Ava pulled the ribbon on her chemise with shaking hands. She was sure he'd think she was fat because she did have wide hips. An hourglass figure her seamstress in New York had said. She'd thought that a good thing until now.

Lucky came to her and put his hands on her shoulders.

"Don't be frightened of me. I'm just a man."

He held her close for a few minutes. She was sure he was trying to ease her fear of him, but that was not the case.

"Better?"

"Not really. I'm trying so hard not to be

afraid, but I can't deny that I am and apparently I can't control my own responses to you."

"I don't want you to control your responses to me, but I don't want your response to me to be fear. I want you to look forward to our times together. Come now let me help you."

He removed the ribbon and pulled open her chemise.

"Beautiful. I knew you would be lovely all over, not just your face."

The words thrilled her, sending shivers up her back. She ducked her head and stared at her hands.

"You really think I'm beautiful?"

He placed his knuckle under her chin and raised her head until she looked in his eyes.

"Yes, I do."

"But I don't look anything like Delilah."

"And I didn't marry her, I married you."

"Would you have married me if I was not fair of face?"

"Yes, I would have. I made a bargain and I always keep my word. I just feel I'm extremely fortunate you're beautiful not plain."

He looked deep in her eyes and lifted his hand to touch her left breast.

She closed her eyes, reveling in the caress.

His hand was gentle, tentative even. Not what she expected of a man she'd kept at bay for hours.

"Jane. Look at me."

She heard the whispered words, wished he could use her real name in these intimate moments, but she opened her eyes, saw his smile and smiled back.

He lowered his head and took her lips with his, softly at first then harder.

His lips left hers only long enough for his hands to pull the ribbon on her bloomers. Then he knelt before her as he pushed them down her legs.

"Step out, please."

Her embarrassment growing as she realized he could see her…there.

He started to rise and stopped half-way up grabbed her by the hips and kissed her mons.

She gasped.

"Lucky! What are you doing?"

She pushed away his head.

"Ah, too soon? But I couldn't resist."

He stood, wrapped his arms around her waist and kissed her.

She couldn't help but close her eyes and marvel at the feelings he elicited.

He walked her backwards until she reached the side of the bed. Then he leaned her backward holding her with one arm and bracing himself with the other until they reached the mattress.

Lucky kissed her lips, her neck, her breasts and worked his way down to her mons. With each kiss he left a burning trail of fire and her womanly parts were alive, wanting more.

"Please, Lucky, help me. Tell me this is not all."

"There's more."

And he showed her. By the time he was done, she'd shattered in a million brilliant pieces.

Her breath slowed, she looked up at him and smiled.

"That was wonderful."

"I'm glad you liked it. Now comes my turn."

He rose over her then covered her, loving her as she'd never in her life been loved before. The pain Jeffrey had told her about was minor and short-lived due she was sure, to Lucky's ministrations beforehand.

Suddenly, he shouted and then he lay upon her...spent.

She wrapped her arms around him, not wanting him to move, not wanting the real world to enter. But it must.

"Lucky."

The single word wheezed out.

"Hmm."

"You're heavy."

"Ah, so I am."

He rolled over and took her with him.

"Well, what do you think of having relations?"

She touched him. Spread her fingers through the sparse hair on his chest and watched it curl around them. She ran her hands over his chest and arms wondering at the muscles there.

"The first part is definitely better than the second part, though even that wasn't what I was led to believe. I'm sure I have you to thank for that."

He looked sated with just a curve to his lips.

"I'm glad you enjoyed it. I intend to

have relations with you as often as we are able."

"Really?" She was sore and still felt him within her, filling her. "You must be kidding me. I'll never survive."

Lucky lay back on the pillows and laughed himself silly.

What have I signed up for?

CHAPTER 6

The next day Ava went to work cleaning the kitchen. She scrubbed the stove with lye soap and a steel brush until most of the grime was off. Then she cleaned the counters with the soap and a regular scrub brush. By the time she was done, her apron was nearly as black as her sleeves would have been if she hadn't rolled them high above her elbow.

She fixed a pot of coffee, about the only staple she could find, and sat at the table, resting after her endeavors.

"Wow. You've made quite a difference in this place."

She looked up at Lucky's voice. He stood in the entry way with his hands on his hips and a wide smile. She still couldn't really believe this gorgeous man was her husband. The thought made her warm inside and she smiled back.

"Thanks. I've had to work hard that's for sure. This apron will never come clean and

I'm tossing it in the trash after I bathe. How do we do that? Do you have a tub somewhere?"

"Yes. Usually I take one here in the kitchen."

He pointed to the center of the room.

"That makes sense. Where are your buckets to heat the water?"

He walked outside and came back in carrying four metal buckets.

The sink had a pump so at least she didn't have to go out to get water.

Lucky went back out and returned carrying a long metal tub.

"Here you go."

"I'll get clean clothes from upstairs. Will you make sure no one enters while I'm in the tub?"

"It will be my pleasure. I'll even scrub your back for you."

She cocked her head and smiled.

"That would be very nice."

"I'm surprised I thought you would be…shyer."

She shrugged.

"You've seen all of me, actually more of me than I've ever seen myself, I think at this point the cats out of the bag and isn't going back in."

He laughed.

"Yes, I suppose you're right about that. You have an amusing way of looking at things."

"Jeffrey and I had to grow up fast and we had only each other so I may not act like other women would in my situation." She jutted her chin. "If you don't like that, that's too bad."

His fingers tightened and he pulled at her shoulders..

She put her arms between them.

"You'll get filthy. I've got grease from the stove on me."

"Do you want me to get you a dress?"

"Yes, that would be nice. The lavender one I got married in, please."

He let go of her and turned toward the door.

"I'll be right back."

Ava pumped the water and filled the buckets, putting all four on the stove to heat.

A few minutes later, Lucky entered with a lavender dress draped over his arm and a stern look on his face.

Her smile faded when she realized what lavender dress he was carrying.

"That's not the dress I wore to get married."

"No. It's the one you wore to get here. What's in the secret pockets?"

"None of your business."

She stood straight, her hands fisted at her sides. Her stomach roiled and she felt like she would throw up.

"You married me. Everything is my business."

He turned the dress inside out and pulled a knife from the sheath at his waist.

"No!"

She thrust out her hands and stepped forward.

"Please. No."

"Tell me what's in it."

"All right. It's full of gems. Diamonds, rubies, emeralds but mostly sapphires."

He narrowed his eyes. "Where did you get them? Did you steal them? Is that why you became a mail-order bride?"

"No. They're mine. Jeffrey gave them to me. But you're right, they are the reason I became a bride."

"Jeffrey? Your dead brother?"

She nodded.

"Yes. Please sit. I'll tell you

everything."

Ava poured them both a cup of coffee. They sat at the table.

Tears formed in her eyes. Telling Lucky about him, made him real and she missed him.

She sniffled.

Lucky handed her his clean handkerchief.

"I told you Jeffrey was an archeologist. That wasn't a lie. His last dig was in Peru. He told me he found an Incan burial chamber and all those gems were within. The agreement he had with the government was he could keep half of what he found in exchange for excavating the tombs."

"I thought he was dead."

"He is. He died on my sofa, the day before I left New York."

Her voice trembled and she had to stop and take deep breaths before she could continue.

"I had to leave him without burying him properly. He made me promise I would get out, get away."

"Why?"

"Because he was murdered. Poisoned by a knife wound in the side. He told me even if I got the wound to close, the poison would kill him anyway."

Ava hadn't let herself mourn for her brother and now the tears were falling like rivers down her cheeks.

Lucky reached over and placed his hand on hers and squeezed. He didn't say anything and she was glad because once she started she had to tell the whole story.

"Jeffrey was afraid whoever killed him would come after you?"

She wiped her eyes and then her nose.

"Yes. This man didn't know about me, but I wasn't hiding then, so he could have found out about me, I suppose from other people that Jeffrey and I knew, perhaps from Jeffrey's other colleagues. And Jeffrey wrote to me while he was in Peru. He was there for two years on this dig."

"Who is *he*?"

She took a deep breath.

"His name is Emmett Walsh. He's a rival archeologist. He told Jeffrey the gems were his. Jeffrey disagreed."

Lucky caressed her hand.

He wanted her to keep talking and was urging her to do so with his caresses. Letting her know she was safe.

"Do you know when your brother was stabbed? How fast acting was the poison? Would this Walsh person have been able to follow him?"

"I don't know. I think he was stabbed when he was in New York City. The wound was still bleeding when he came to me. Jeffrey was fairly certain that Walsh hadn't followed him."

"So you came here to hide. What else don't I know about you? I don't suppose your name is Jane Smith."

Ava shook her head. She needed to protect him. If Emmet Walsh found her...

"No. I'm Ava Lewis. I'm sorry Lucky. I'll leave. I don't want to bring this down on you. If I leave now, I can hopefully get to San Francisco and disappear there or find a ship—"

Her heart ached in her chest. She didn't know that heart break was a physical feeling. Maybe she'd never been in love before.

"You're not leaving. You're my wife... *Ava*."

"By using my real name as my middle name I was trying to make sure our marriage was legal, but that probably didn't make any difference. We're not really married. You can contact Mrs. Selby and get another bride."

"I like you. I'm not looking for a way out of this marriage…just a way to keep you safe. In public and to everyone we know you will be Jane, but when we are together and it's just you and me, you will be Ava. It's a beautiful name."

She wiped the tears from her eyes.

"Why are you being so kind? I deceived you."

"You had good reason. I don't like what you did, but I understand it, more than you know."

She reached for the dress.

"Can I have my dress now?"

He pulled the garment out of her reach.

"I'll get you another one. This one needs to be put back and left alone. These pockets make a good hiding place."

"I don't know about that, you found them."

He stood and shook his head.

"Only because I was so stupid. I remembered the frayed cuffs of the dress you wore and forgot that we'd bought you another one. I assume you will make jewelry from the gems."

"Yes, that's my plan. Jeffrey would have wanted that. I want each of the creations to be special, something he would either have worn or bought for a lady to wear. I want to set up a shop here in Central City but be able to sell them in New York and for sure in Denver."

"You've thought about this a lot."

"All the way here from New York. That's a long trip."

He laid the dress over his arm.

"You had a lot of opportunities to get off the train or the stagecoach and start a new life somewhere. Why didn't you?"

"I don't know." She looked up at him. "As you said, I made a bargain and I keep my word. Those stones notwithstanding, I'm an honest person."

"As far as we know, Jeffrey found the stones and owned them so you own them now, but we should prepare for this Emmett Walsh person to show up looking for you."

"Why? No one, except you, knows I became a bride or where I went."

Lucky sat back at the table with her.

"What about Mrs. Selby?"

"She knows me as Jane Smith not Ava

Lewis."

"You might be surprised. He could have had you followed to the matchmaker, even to here and you wouldn't know."

She cocked her head and narrowed her eyes.

"How would you know these things?"

"Let's just say I used to make my living in the shadows, making sure people weren't aware I was there, until it was too late."

"I'm not sure if I should be scared, fascinated or reassured. I'm definitely fascinated and not scared because I know you would never hurt me. So that must mean I'm reassured."

"You have a roundabout way of coming to a conclusion."

He stood and turned to leave.

"I assume you still want a bath and clean clothes."

"Oh yes, please. Will you make sure no one else comes in? Or are you disgusted with me?"

He turned back.

"I'm not disgusted. Never. I think you're very brave to have come here alone, knowing you carried a fortune in gems with you."

She relaxed against the chair.

"Thank you."

"You're welcome. I'll be right back."

Ava poured two of the buckets of hot water into the tub and then pumped cold water into one of the buckets and dumped that into the bath. She checked the temperature and it was still a little too hot, so she added more cold water.

When Lucky returned he was carrying the correct lavender dress.

"We must get you some new clothes."

"Let's wait and see what Alice sends. Then we'll know what else I need."

She took off the apron.

He sighed.

"All right. We'll wait, but we could see if there is a ready-to-wear dress at the mercantile. It would be something for everyday or that you could use to clean in since the one you're wearing seems to be done for."

She looked down at herself and saw that the apron had not protected her dress from the grime after all.

She sighed and slumped her shoulders.

"Well, I guess we'll be heading out to the mercantile after I bathe. Would you turn your back, please?"

"Why?"

"So I can get into the tub."

"You know I've seen every part of you and will see you when you're in the tub."

"I know, but undressing in front of you still seems…well, I can't explain it."

He reached toward her.

"How about if I help you undress? Would you feel more at ease?"

"Heavens, no. I'll do it."

She unbuttoned her blouse and shed it, followed in quick succession with the rest of her clothes. When the last piece was off, she hurried into the tub.

"I forgot the soap. Will you hand me that bar of lye soap."

"Lye soap? Are you trying to take your skin off?"

"No, but I forgot to bring my rose soap down with me or a towel and washcloth. Would you get me those things, too?"

She smiled.

"Please."

Lucky took a deep breath.

He let it out slowly like he was attempting to keep control of his temper.

"I'll be right back."

He'd been gone a few minutes when the back door opened and Delilah strode in. She wore her normal red satin dress, black hat with red feathers that matched her dress and acted like she owned the place.

Ava shouted. "Delilah, what are you doing here?"

"I could ask the same of you."

Ava leaned forward to try and cover herself.

"I'm having a bath and you're not welcome here. I suggest you leave before Lucky returns."

Delilah put her hands on her hips.

"I wonder what Lucky would do if he found you drowned in your bath water."

No one, especially this woman would threaten her life and get away with it.

"Come try it?"

Ava stood and got out of the tub.

"Afraid to face me? Happy to say things behind my back but not to my face? Well I'm not afraid to say what I'm thinking. You're a bitch and I won't let you slap me again. Lucky's not here to save you this time."

Delilah's eyes narrowed and she ran at Ava, grabbing her around the waist and knocking them both to the ground.

That was how Lucky found them. Delilah's dress was torn, her hat askew and Ava sitting stark-ass-naked on top of her punching her in the face.

He stared at his wife. She'd taken a few hits herself, he saw that she had a cut above her swollen left eye.

Dropping the dress in his hands, he plucked Ava off of Delilah.

"That's enough both of you."

"She threatened to drown me. I'm not going down without a fight."

"So I see." *Who would have thought my little bride is a brawler?* "Delilah, if you know what's good for you you'll get out of here before I let my wife finish what she started."

Delilah pulled on her dress, wiped her lip, looked down at her hand, saw the blood and frowned.

"I'm leaving but you better watch your back, Jane Madigan."

The woman stalked through the back door, out of the kitchen.

Lucky turned Ava in his arms and examined her face.

"Your beautiful face will look like hell

for a few days. She landed a good one on your eye."

"She got in a few lucky punches, but she wasn't prepared for someone whose brother taught her to street fight."

"Sounds like Jeffrey taught you a lot of things most girls, and women, wouldn't know. For now though you need to get back in the tub. I'll get the hot water and warm it up a little."

"Thanks."

She walked out of his embrace, head high and slipped back into the tub.

"Will you still wash my back?"

"Of course. It needs it more now that you've wallowed in the dirt on the floor."

She looked down at herself and saw that her breasts and stomach were covered in mud, from where her wet body had met the dirty floor.

Fifteen minutes later she stood in the tub while Lucky poured water from a bucket over her head to rinse the suds from her hair.

"There you, go. All clean."

He'd put down a towel by the tub so she wouldn't slip or have to step into a muddy mess.

She slipped out of the tub and reached

for the drying cloth in his hand.

He pulled it out of her reach and shook his finger.

"Let me. Here's one for your hair. I'll do your body."

She wrapped her hair in the towel.

Starting with her arms he worked his way down her body, spending a particularly long time on her breasts and her mons.

When he was done, she was like a bowl of jelly with her legs barely holding her up.

"You are not allowed to dry me anymore. I'm ready to make love to you and we have too many things to do yet today."

He frowned.

"That was not well done of me. You're probably still sore from last night."

"There was some soreness, but the bath helped that. By tonight I should be just fine I would think."

He grinned.

"Then I shall think only of tonight."

As will I, though I would never admit it to him. His head is big enough.

She smiled. Then she remembered Delilah and wondered what the woman had been doing here. What would she do next?

CHAPTER 7

December 13, 1869
The Colton home

Ava and Rita sat in the parlor sipping tea and talking when Ava finally told her the reason for the visit.

"Rita, I have a proposition. You know I make jewelry, and I need gold to do that. Since Jack has the biggest gold mine in town, I thought you and I could go into business. I'd provide the gems and labor to make the jewelry. You would provide the gold and be the saleswoman and we split everything fifty-fifty. I know you were a dancer and that you might not know the first thing about selling jewelry, but you like jewelry and I've always found that the best salesmen are people who love the product. What do you think?"

"I've been looking for something to keep me busy. Let me talk to Jack about it, though I'm sure he'll say yes. We will need a store, just a small one, to sell the product. I think I know of a place and it's on Main Street, too. It was one of the assayer's offices in town, so it may already have a safe to protect the jewels, gold and finished pieces."

Ava was thrilled Rita agreed.

"You're right. We'll definitely need a safe. Do you want to go with me to look at the shop?"

"Of course."

Rita squealed a little bit.

"This will be so much fun."

"I hope you're right and that we get lots of orders and lots of visitors. I want us both to stay busy and happy. I don't know about you, but I'm about ready to go crazy. There is nothing for me to do. I already scrubbed the kitchen so I'd have a place to cook."

Ava grinned.

"Lucky seems happy with my efforts so far. He loves my bread, anyway, though I had to make some adjustments for the altitude here."

"I don't cook, so I wouldn't have any idea about the changes needed. Mrs. Potts would be devastated if I started cooking. Besides, I'm a terrible cook."

Ava laughed.

"Well, I'm a decent cook and now that we have a place to eat, I'd like for you and Jack to come to dinner...er...supper."

"I knew what you meant. In New York the meal is dinner, here it's supper and dinner is at noon or one o'clock. Sometimes things are so confusing."

Ava stood and started toward the door.

"Yes, they are. I should go now. Lucky will be done meeting with his managers and probably wonder where I am. I left him a note, though."

From the hallway they hear Lucky's voice.

"Thank you Mrs. Bates, I know my way to the parlor."

Rita grimaced.

"Uh oh, he sounds angry. Do you want me to leave you two alone?"

"No, he'll hold his temper until we're on the way home. See you for supper tonight at six."

Ava hoped she was right and Lucky wouldn't lose his temper.

"We'll be there."

Lucky strode into the room.

"Ladies."

"Why Lucky, we weren't expecting you," said Rita.

He stared at Ava.

"Obviously, but you should have been. Jane isn't supposed to leave without telling me, are you, my dear?"

Ava let out a sigh.

"I expected to be back before you finished your meeting. Since I didn't make that you can walk me home."

"Yes, and we can have a little talk along the way."

"Fine but don't you want to know why I came to see Rita?"

"Because she's your friend?"

"Yes, she's my friend, my only friend, but that isn't why I came to see her. I want us to go into business together."

He lifted his eyebrows.

"You and Rita? But she's a dancer."

Rita put her hands on her hips.

"I'll have you know, sir, that I have more talents than just dancing."

Lucky ran his hand behind his neck.

"Rita, I didn't mean anything bad. It is just an observation."

Ava rolled her eyes and then told Lucky the plan.

"Rita's telling Jack about it when he gets home to see if he's willing to supply the gold. I'll need some equipment. Oh, and Rita knows of a shop that might be available, the assayers shop on Main Street. Do you know it?"

Lucky nodded and crossed his arms over his chest.

"I know the place and she's right. It would be perfect for you. We'll go see it on the way home. The building is just a few doors down from the Golden Spike."

"Are you ready then? I'm anxious to see the place."

Ava stood and Rita followed.

"Jane, this will be so much fun. You wait and see. You'll have the most successful jewelry store in Central City and before you know it you'll be getting orders from Golden City, too."

"That would be wonderful," said Ava. "Is there another jewelry store in Central City?"

I hope I can sell to Denver and New York eventually, too.

"Well, no, but there will be," said Rita. "And you'll be the best."

"Shall we go?" asked Lucky.

"Yes, I'm ready."

She hugged Rita.

"See you soon."

When they were about half way down the driveway, Lucky took Ava's hand.

"Ava, do you understand why I need to know where you are? I worry about you. I worry that Emmett Walsh character has found you, and I'm afraid he will regardless of the pains you took to get away."

"I'm sorry." She leaned into him as they walked. "I do know that. I guess I hadn't realized how much you worry. I'd think you liked me or something."

"I do like you and you know it, too."

She laughed.

"Yes, but I do enjoy hearing you say it."

They were just a few doors from home when Lucky stopped in front of an empty store. The building was nondescript—just a plain wooden building, painted white like the structures around it. The words *Assayer* were painted in gold letters on the shingle to the left of the door.

Ava peered through the window. The shop appeared to be about ten feet by thirty feet, though that was an estimate because the door behind the counter could be to another room or to the outside.

"This place looks wonderful. When can I go inside?"

"I'll get in touch with the owner as soon as I can. He lives in Denver."

She stood on tip-toe and kissed his cheek.

"Thank you. Shall we go home? I can prepare lunch or dinner or whatever you call the midday meal."

Lucky laughed.

"Don't get so flustered, honey. You can call it whatever you want."

"Then I choose lunch. That's what I'm used to. So what do you want for lunch?"

He put his arm around her shoulders as they walked to the Golden Spike.

"What are my options?"

"I have stew and I can make fresh rolls. The dough was starting to rise when I left. It should be ready to form and bake. Do you want rolls or would you rather have a loaf? On the other hand I can fry a couple of steaks."

"Rolls and stew, please."

"I asked Rita and Jack to come for dinner tonight. I'm fixing a beef roast. I got a nice one from the butcher yesterday."

Lucky gave her shoulders a squeeze.

"I do believe you're becoming used to the fact this is your home and you're not leaving any time soon, or at all, without me."

She leaned into him.

"I'm coming around to that idea, as long as I'm not putting anyone else in danger."

"Are you happy here, Ava?"

"Yes, for the most part even though our marriage isn't valid."

"It is valid. We were married and are living as man and wife. Everyone knows us as man and wife."

Her throat grew tight and her breathing wispy.

"What happens when you meet the woman you *can* love, who makes you forget whatever it is that keeps you from loving me? What happens then?"

He slowed his strides.

"That can never happen. Trust me."

"I do trust you, I just wish I could believe you about this, but I know that someday you'll find the one you love."

"So you think I'll keep looking? That I won't honor my vows to you? What about you? What if you find the person you love?"

She stopped walking and looked up at him.

"But I thought you knew by now. I have, though I'm trying my best not to. I don't want to love someone who doesn't love me, and yet I don't seem to have a lot of choice."

"Then why do you keep saying things like 'I can still leave'?"

Ava struggled to get out the words, the pain in her heart almost too much to bear at the thought that he would leave her.

"Because I want you to be happy. If you're not happy with me then I need to leave so you *can* be happy. It's that simple."

He stopped next to her, right outside the Golden Spike, turned her in his arms and kissed her.

"You're a strange woman, Ava Madigan."

"No, I'm just married to a strange man. Let's go upstairs."

Lucky's hand was on the door when they heard her.

Delilah was behind them on the boardwalk.

"So, now it's Ava. I thought your name was Jane."

Ava turned to face her foe, hands fisted.

"Whatever my name, it's none of your business, Delilah. What are you doing here? You know you're not welcome."

"I'm here to see, Pete. But I think your name just became my business. Who are you hiding from *Ava*?"

"Ava is my middle name and what I prefer to go by. So just go away, Delilah, before I swat you like a fly." Ava looked up at Lucky. "Aren't you going to say anything?"

He shook his head and raised his hands in front of him.

"You seem to have things well in hand, my dear."

Delilah jumped on the fact he didn't come to Ava's aid.

"See that? He won't even stand up for you," said Delilah.

Ava frowned. "I don't need him to stand up for me. I can fight my own battles or have you forgotten already. Leave now before I make you sorry you came here today."

Delilah stiffened her stance.

"I'm leaving but only because I have to go to work. I'm not afraid of you *Ava* or Jane or whatever your real name is. But I promise you I will find out."

Delilah pulled up the hood of her cloak so it covered her hair, turned her back on them and walked down the street toward the center of town.

"What are we going to do? The more people who know my real name the easier I'll be to find. And what about Rita?"

"What about Rita?"

"She's supposed to go into business with me. What if—"

"Not here."

He grasped her elbow and escorted into the saloon. They stopped talking before walking into the saloon and up the stairs to their apartment.

Once inside, they hung up their coats and Ava fixed them each a cup of tea. Heating the water on the small two burner stove Lucky installed so she didn't have to go downstairs through the saloon just to get a cup of tea late at night. She was grateful that he'd seen her distress and eased it. She sat at the table across from Lucky, and then got up again, much too agitated to sit. Ava paced between stove and the table.

"So what are we to do about Delilah?"

Lucky put his hands around the cup.

"There's not a lot we can do. I think we should tell our friends, Jack, Rita, Robert and Henry. They can help us."

Ava lifted her hands. "How can they help us? We don't know who they should be looking for."

She stopped pacing.

"I just realized, Delilah can't hurt me. She doesn't know who might be coming either."

She walked back to the table and sat.

"No one knows. All we can do is be prepared for anyone that does come."

"That's true. I still believe we should tell everyone your real name. They should start calling you Ava. Delilah has no power if your name isn't a secret any longer."

"All right. We'll tell everyone."

*****

They decided it was best to do it all at once and invited all of their friends to dinner. Jack and Rita were already coming to dinner that night. Lucky sent boys with invitations to Robert and Henry.

Since she'd cleaned the kitchen, Lucky had had a large, rectangular table that seated eight, made so they could entertain their friends. They just hadn't thought this meeting would be the first use of it.

Jack and Rita were the first to arrive. They came in the kitchen door to avoid going through the saloon.

"Something smells wonderful," said Jack.

"Roast beef, with fresh baked rolls, carrots, parsley potatoes," said Ava.

"Let me take your coats," said Lucky.

Jack and Rita took off their coats and handed them to Lucky who hung them on the pegs on the wall by the door to the saloon.

"Would either of you like a drink?" asked Ava. She was so nervous she actually thought about having a stiff drink herself.

"I'll take some of that Jameson Lucky keeps for special guests."

"What? You think you're special? Rita, of course, but you, Jack?" asked Lucky. "You're fortunate that I brought a bottle in just for tonight."

"Just pour the damn, I mean, darn whiskey. Excuse me, ladies," Jack ducked his head toward Ava and Rita.

Lucky laughed and gave Jack a glass containing two fingers of the prized whiskey.

"Robert and Henry are joining us tonight," said Lucky.

Ava checked the gravy sitting as a low simmer on the stove.

"Rita, will you help me set the table, please?"

"Sure."

She handed Rita the new pottery plates while Ava got the cutlery. She had bought everything new. Lucky hadn't had a plate or knife or fork in the house.

Robert and Henry arrived almost at the same time. Lucky hung their coats next to Jack and Rita's, then got them each a drink.

"Shall we all sit? Lucky and I have something to tell you," said Ava.

"If this is where you tell us you're expecting, I already knew," said Rita.

Ava's eyes widened, she looked down and spread her hands over her stomach.

"What? I...I..."

"Ava?" said Lucky softly.

She looked up at him. Tears welling in her eyes.

"I...I don't know. I...I could be. We've been married almost two months."

Lucky picked her up around the waist and swung her in a circle.

He laughed.

"We're having a baby."

Ava wrapped her arms around Lucky's neck, leaned down and touched her lips to her husband's. Happiness filled her. She hadn't even given a thought to being with child, but now that Rita mentioned it, she couldn't get the thought out of her head.

"Come on you two. That's enough. If you didn't bring us here...hey wait a minute," said Jack. "Why'd you call her Ava? She's Jane."

Lucky let Ava slide down his body and then with an arm still around her waist, he hugged her close.

"I want you all to meet my wife-to-be. Ava Lewis. We're getting married as soon as she says yes."

"What?" asked Jack.

"What do you mean wife-to-be?" asked Henry, a frown on his face. "You've been married for two months."

"Well," said Lucky. "We've been sort of married. Jane's real name is Ava Lewis. We've presented ourselves as married but that may not be enough for us to be legally wed."

"So we're getting married again, just in

case," said Ava.

"When?" asked Robert with a smile.

"Just as soon as the preacher will have us. My guess would be tomorrow."

"Let us know what time and we'll be there," said Rita.

"Good, because we want you and Jack to stand up for us," said Ava. Her heart pounded in her chest. So much to take in, expecting and getting married—she closed her eyes and took a deep breath.

"Then why don't we all go together. I'll bring the carriage about ten and we'll go see the reverend," said Jack.

"That would be great. Now that we have that settled, shall we eat?" asked Lucky. "Ava has a great dinner prepared. I've discovered my wife is a terrific cook. You're in for a pleasant surprise."

"Thank you, Lucky. I'm glad you appreciate my cooking efforts."

Lucky grinned.

"I do, my dear. I most assuredly do."

Ava and Rita put all the food on the table and Ava set the roast beef in front of Lucky to cut.

"This is great Jane...I mean Ava," said Robert.

"Remembering to call you Ava will take some time," said Henry. "We just got used to Lucky having a wife named Jane."

"I know and I'm sorry about that but I have my reasons for deceiving you. Delilah has thought to hurt me by revealing my secret, so the only thing to do was to get ahead of her and make the announcement myself. You are the only people I care about here and I wouldn't have her hurt you or me with her meanness. I want you all to be safe. There is a man after me and I don't want you to be injured by getting in his way. He wants something from me that I'm not giving him. His name is Emmett Walsh. If you come across him for any reason, let me or Lucky know, but don't let him know that you know me."

"We'll do it," said Jack. "You're a good woman, Ava. I'm sure whatever your reasons for wanting to avoid this man are good ones and you'll reveal them to us at the appropriate time."

"Thank you, Jack. I will. I promise."

I will reveal all to these people, my friends, when the time is right and the danger has passed. I don't want any of them to be hurt.

CHAPTER 8

Wednesday, December 15, 1869
The little white church in Blackhawk

"Thanks for seeing us again, Reverend Jenkins," said Ava.

"After what you've told me, how could I not. We must get you married in accordance with the law of the territory. In God's eyes you were married two months ago, but according to the law you are not.

"That's what we were afraid of," said Ava. "I'm so sorry reverend. I was trying to keep everyone safe."

"Knowledge will keep them safe. Remember that, my child."

"Yes, sir," said Ava but she was thinking about what he said. *Is he right? Should I tell them everything? Will that keep them safe?*

"Are you ready to start?"

"Yes, sir," answered Lucky. "The sooner the better."

Rita and Jack stood with them as the reverend repeated the vows from before but using her correct name Ava Marie Lewis. Five minutes later, she was indeed Mrs. Seamus Madigan, legally. No one could use the knowledge of her real name against her now. Ava sighed and leaned into Lucky who was now truly her husband.

*****

Delilah Monroe smoothed the red satin dress over her curves. She had more than her singing voice going for her. She had her body and wasn't afraid to use it to achieve her purpose.

Approaching the two men at the bar of the Longbranch Saloon, she sidled up next to the one in the gray suit. He seemed to be the one in charge.

"I understand you're looking for a woman named Ava Lewis?"

"That's right. Do you know where we can find her?"

"Maybe. Why don't you buy me a drink and we can talk more at that table." She jutted her chin toward the round table at the end of the bar which was kept open for just such a time, so business could be discussed discreetly.

"Joe, a bottle of the best, please."

The bartender put a half-empty bottle of whiskey on the bar along with three shot glasses.

Delilah picked them up on the way to the table.

"Sit, gentlemen. I'm Delilah Monroe, and I'm your new best friend."

She poured them all a shot of bourbon.

The men sat, one on either side of Delilah.

"What do you want Miss Monroe?" asked the man in the gray suit.

"First, to know who you are."

The man looked her up and down.

"Very well. I'm Emmett Walsh and this is my associate Carl Kroger."

"As I said, you are looking for Ava Lewis, is that right?"

"That is correct."

Delilah looked at her hand pretending to examine her nails. Her heart pounded and her stomach turned. This could be the big one. Enough to get out of Central City for good.

"What would you give to find this woman?"

"What do you want, Miss Monroe?"

She looked up.

"I want out of this place. I want one thousand dollars and I'll give you the name and her location as well."

"That's a lot of money."

"That's a lot of information for you."

"How about five hundred dollars?"

"How about a thousand and you can stay with me while you're here."

She leaned over so he could get a good look at what he would be giving up.

"You drive a hard bargain, Miss Monroe. You have a deal. Shall we drink on it?"

Delilah drank her shot without taking her gaze off Emmett Walsh.

"I'd like half the money up front and the second half when I take you to her."

Emmett narrowed his gaze, then reached into his suit jacket and took out a fat wallet. He removed the cash, peeled off five one-hundred dollar bills and handed it to her.

She eyed the money, folded it and stuffed the cash down the front of her dress where she was sure not to lose it.

"Her name now is Jane Madigan. She's the wife of the owner of the Golden Spike Saloon, Lucky Madigan. They live in an apartment above the saloon, but *Ava* spends a lot of her time alone in the kitchen. She likes to bake apparently."

"How did you come by this information, Miss Monroe?"

"I used to work at the Golden Spike before I let my tongue get away from me and insulted the owner's wife. I happened to be visiting one of the girls who still works there when I heard, Lucky, call her Ava as I was leaving the saloon."

"That's very good information, Miss Monroe."

He peeled off the additional five one-hundred dollar bills.

"Worth every penny."

Not that I care what he calls me, but it does make sleeping with him a little less like business if he doesn't call me Miss Monroe.

"Do you think we can be less formal? You call me Delilah and I call you Emmett?"

"As you wish. I'll be visiting you tonight. Where do you live?"

"Here in room six, upstairs. I'll be back in my room after one o'clock in the morning."

"Very good. I shall see you then."

Emmett and Carl stood and left the saloon

Delilah went up to her room and hid the money beneath her bed under a loose floorboard.

*****

Ava turned over in bed and leaned on her elbow. "Good morning, Mr. Madigan."

"Good morning, the real Mrs. Madigan."

He leaned up and kissed her before moving the blankets away and putting his arm up so she could cuddle. She rolled over, putting her head on his arm and her arm on his chest, where she let her fingers play with the soft hair there.

"I am aren't I? Really married to you?"

"Yes, you are and none too soon now that you're having my baby."

This was not the declaration of love Ava had hoped to hear, but she supposed that was as close as she would get. They'd only been married for a couple of months. Just because she loved him, didn't mean he was in love with her, at least not yet.

Lucky wasn't giving up his heart, not to her or anyone. If he asked, she'd tell him she'd take good care of his heart, that it was safe with her, but he didn't ask. Didn't want to know. He painted her with the same brush as every other woman. But every other woman didn't love him completely to the distraction of everything else.

Ava crawled out of bed and put on her robe. No one was about in the saloon this early in the morning, no reason to get completely dressed, though she did throw on her coat over her robe.

"What would you like for breakfast?"

Lucky's gaze traveled up and down her body.

"You."

She smiled and shook her head.

"That's what you say every morning."

He grinned.

"And I mean it every morning."

Ava went down the stairs. The stark emptiness of the saloon in the mornings when it had been so full of life the night before always seemed surreal to her.

She went into the kitchen and put on a pot of coffee, got eggs and bacon from the icebox and started the bacon frying. Cutting four thick slices from the bread she baked yesterday, she put another pan on the stove, buttered both sides of the bread and put the slices in the skillet to brown.

Ava then sat at the table with a copy of the Rocky Mountain News from last week and waited for the food to cook.

A knock sounded on the back door.

She glanced up and then ignored it. The only people she wanted to see knew that they needed to come through the front unless expected and she wasn't expecting anyone. The glass in the door shattered and she was up like a shot, running for Lucky. Instinct told her this wasn't Delilah, this wasn't a fight she could win. She knew in those few split seconds that Walsh had found her and she needed to run.

She screamed as she entered the saloon.

"Lucky!"

Several sets of heavy footsteps hurried behind her.

She ran for the stairs and had gone up two when she was grabbed by the waist from behind and pulled down.

Lucky appeared at the top, stark naked, a knife in one hand and a revolver in the other.

Ava heard the whoosh of the knife flying past her head into her would be assailant.

The man yelled and let her go.

She took the stairs two at a time.

Shots sounded from above and below her.

Hitting the landing at the top of the staircase, she ran for Lucky.

He stood legs braced apart, arm extended and fired again and again without return shots sounding.

"Get inside," he hissed.

No need to tell her twice. She ran through the door into their apartment.

Lucky followed, shut the door behind him and locked it.

He was beside her in an instant.

"Are you all right?"

"Yes, I'm fine. Thank you for saving me." She panted, trying to catch her breath and collapsed on the sofa. Her heart raced and beat so hard she thought the organ would explode from her chest.

"That's what husband's are good for."

"That had to have been Emmett Walsh. Who else would want to abduct me?"

"There were two men. But how do they know you're here? We only married yesterday."

"The informant had to be Delilah. Somehow she found them and told them where I'd be. It couldn't have been anyone else."

"You're right. I'll be having a few words with her today after I take you to Jack and Rita's place."

"Why am I going to their home?"

"You're safer there than here. Too many people in the saloon. Too many unknowns. At Jack and Rita's, an enemy can be seen coming a long way off."

"I'm taking the jewels with me. That's what he wants and he won't get them. Jeffrey died for those stones. He owned them legally and now they are mine."

"I understand. Wear your old dress with them safely sewn inside. You can change into a more stylish gown at Jack's. Get dressed now."

She slid the robe off her shoulders, letting it fall to the floor, and then went to the bureau for her undergarments, followed by her dress and half boots.

Her heart was slowing down and she was feeling safe again.

"You made quite the picture of an avenging angel...naked as a jaybird wielding that knife and then the gun. Where did your blade hit the person holding me?"

"In the left shoulder."

"Wow. That's very good."

He frowned and shook his head.

"I need to practice more."

"Why? It's amazing you wounded him like you did."

"Not good enough. I was aiming for his head."

"Oh, I see what you mean. Still you were wonderful. Thank you."

"Of course, I'll save you. You're my wife. You carry my child."

He pulled on his clothes while he talked to her.

She again had hoped he would tell her he loved her and that was why he saved her. But she was disappointed. Lucky didn't love her. She'd better get used to the idea. He was her husband, her protector, the father of her child and nothing more.

Ava felt her heart break but resigned herself to the sentiment or lack thereof.

"I'm ready."

He sat on the bed pulling on his boots.

"Did you pack your valise?"

She picked the bag off the bed and headed toward the door.

"Yes. It's ready to go."

He held his hand out for the valise.

"Good. Let's leave. I want you safe as soon as possible. And it'll be dangerous the whole walk to Jack's."

She handed him the bag and then turned to go out the door.

He held her back and went first, checking the floor below for intruders.

"Okay, let's go."

They descended the stairs.

"Do you smell that? Breakfast!"

Ava hurried to the kitchen, Lucky following. She picked up a couple of pot holders and moved the skillets to the sink and left them. They wouldn't burn down the saloon.

They went back out and at the bottom of the stairs was Lucky's knife, covered in the kidnapper's blood.

"I'll have to clean this at Jack's."

"I'm glad you're so good with a knife. Where'd you learn?"

"I've been practicing with a knife since I was a boy. But I honed my skills in the army."

"What did you do?"

He was quiet for far too long.

"Lucky?"

"I don't want to talk about that now. Let

the dead rest."

What an odd comment to make.

"All right I won't mention it to you again."

"Thank you."

Lucky stopped at the door leading to the outside from the saloon, opened it cautiously and peered out. Then he opened the door wide and walked out, holding out his hand to her.

She grasped his hand and walked out, looking all around for men who might be watching, waiting for her to leave.

When they got outside they turned left when leaving the building.

"Do you know how to ride?"

"Well, no, but I could ride with you. Where are we going? This isn't the way to Jack's."

"I'm renting a carriage at the livery. Riding in it will be much safer than walking."

Lucky held the valise in his left hand and held her hand with his right.

If she hadn't been so scared she would have protested his walking at such a fast clip.

They reached the livery quickly. The

business was only four blocks from the Golden Spike.

Lucky went to the door and pounded on it until someone answered. The man appeared to have been asleep before Lucky started pounding on the door.

"What do you want at this hour?"

"I'm sorry to get you up Nate, but I need a carriage and I need it quickly. I'll help you harness the horses."

"Okay, Lucky. Come on in."

Ava kept looking behind them making sure no one was following them but hadn't seen a soul even looking their way. A couple of drunks stumbled out of one of the saloons that was opened twenty-four hours a day.

When the buggy was ready, Lucky helped her into it and then he climbed in next to her. Nate opened the doors and they hurried through. When Lucky turned on to Main Street headed for Jack and Rita's, Ava relaxed a bit.

"When this is all over you can teach me how to ride."

"You still thinking about that? You can't ride while you're expecting."

She looked at him. "Why not?"

He looked at her like she was an idiot.

"It's not good for the baby."

She turned her head until she was looking straight ahead. "I think that's a bunch of nonsense. Besides, we don't even know for sure that I'm expecting until the doctor checks me out."

He put his hand on her knee.

"But you could be. I'm not taking any risks."

"Then shouldn't you be carrying me everywhere? I might trip and fall."

He stopped and turned toward her.

"You're right."

She put up her hand.

"Stop. That's ridiculous. We'll ask Rita. She's expecting, due in about four months. The doctor must have told her what to do and not to do. You don't see Jack carrying her everywhere."

"That's true and she's farther along that you are."

"See. You're being crazy."

Ten minutes later they were knocking on Jack and Rita's door.

The heavy mahogany door opened and Mrs. Bates appeared.

"Mr. and Mrs. Madigan. Please come in. I'll tell Jack you're here."

"Thanks, Mrs. Bates. Where is he?" asked Lucky

"In the dining room taking his breakfast," answered Mrs. Bates, pointing down the hall. "Would you like me to take your valise for you?"

"No thank you, Mrs. Bates. We'll keep it with us."

"As you wish." She nodded and waved her arm toward the hallway.

"We'll find our own way. Come on, Ava. You're probably hungry, too."

Lucky grabbed her hand and practically dragged her down the hall, barely giving her a chance to see the lovely Persian carpets.

"I think I'm still too scared to be hungry."

"But you need to eat to keep up your strength for you and the babe."

"Let's just go see Jack."

Jack looked up and then stood as they entered the dining room.

"Well, hello you two. Grab some breakfast on your way over.

He pointed to the side board.

Lucky put down the valise against the wall just inside the door.

"Don't mind if I do," said Lucky.

He walked to the buffet, grabbed a plate and piled it high with food.

"Come on, Ava. You need to eat," said Lucky.

"Oh, all right."

She followed him and grabbed a plate and dished up a spoonful of scrambled eggs, a slice of ham and two slices of toast.

"You're lucky," said Jack. "Rita was sick as a dog her first couple of months."

Ava swallowed her first bite of scrambled eggs and ham. "I'm healthy as a horse. I can eat just about—"

Her eyes widened and she looked around for something…

"Over by the window. Large vase on the floor," said Jack nonchalantly. Then he got up and pulled the cord to call Mrs. Bates.

Ava ran for the vase and then puked up her guts.

"Ava!"

Lucky followed and placed his hand on her back.

When she was done, she sat on the floor for a few minutes.

Lucky squatted next to her. "Are you all right?"

His eyebrows were furrowed and he

frowned.

She lifted her hand and caressed his face.

"Yes, I appear to be done now," said Ava.

Mrs. Bates came in saw the way of things and left.

"Good. You scared me to death," said Lucky.

"Don't worry the baby is fine."

He looked at her, lifted an eyebrow and cocked his head and she thought maybe, just maybe he was concerned for her.

He shook his head and narrowed his eyes as if trying to understand her. Then he looked away and when he turned back to her the intense gaze was gone.

"Good. That's good."

"First time she's gotten sick?" asked Jack.

"Yes. Why? Is it normal?" asked Lucky.

Mrs. Bates returned with a large glass of water and a couple of hand towels.

"Thank you, Mrs. Bates," said Ava.

"My pleasure, Mrs. Madigan."

"Apparently it is. The doctor wasn't concerned about it. Just said to make sure she ate enough later. We finally found that dry toast and tea stayed down. That's still what Rita has for breakfast...just in case. You'll find some on the sideboard."

Lucky walked over to the buffet, placed two pieces of dry toast on a plate and poured a cup of tea. He took it all back to Ava's seat next to him at the table.

She finally sat up away from the vase, fairly sure that nothing else would be coming up.

"Feel better?" asked Lucky. He squatted next to her.

"Yes, thank you."

"Here." He handed her a damp napkin.

She ran the cloth over her lips and around her mouth, making sure no sick remained.

"Ready to stand?"

"Yes."

"Let me help you."

Lucky stood and held out his hand.

She grasped it and he pulled her to her feet and into his arms.

"Are you sure you're feeling all right? Need to lie down?"

"No, I'm fine. Thank you for asking."

Ava watched as Rita sailed into the room, light as if she was still dancing.

"What did I miss?"

CHAPTER 9

"I just got sick." Ava pressed a hand to her stomach.

"Oh, that explains why you're so pale," said Rita.

"Her first time," said Jack.

Rita nodded.

"You'll be glad to know that the sickness goes away after a few months."

"Months!" said Ava.

My god I can't do this for months! I won't survive.

"Yes, but don't worry. You won't throw up as long as you eat something light first thing." She turned to Jack. "Did you tell them about the dry toast and tea?"

He nodded. "Lucky got some for her. She'll be right as rain in a bit."

Rita seated herself in the chair to Jack's right.

"The first time it happened, I was scared to death. I thought something was wrong with the baby."

"Oh, well I'm glad to know that this sickness is normal, but I'd like it better if I didn't feel sick."

Rita nodded.

"It's called morning sickness and most women have it for the first three months or so. Sometimes longer. Some poor women have it for the whole nine months."

"Oh, how awful," said Ava. She couldn't imagine having this for the entire pregnancy. How miserable that would be.

Lucky held Ava's chair out for her and then sat in his own on the left side of Jack's.

"Now that Rita is here we want to ask you if we can stay with you for a while, hence the valise."

Lucky pointed at the bag next to the wall.

"What's happened?" Jack set his cutlery on the table giving Lucky his full attention.

"We had early morning visitors who tried to kidnap Ava and tried to kill me."

Jack sat up straight.

"What? Why?"

Ava looked at Lucky and then told her friends about the gems. The whole story from when Jeffrey came back into Ava's life. Telling the story to Jack and Rita brought all her grief to the forefront, holding Jeffrey while he died, having to leave him there so she could run for her life. Tears streamed down her face and she didn't stop them, couldn't have if she'd wanted to and she didn't want to. She wanted to mourn her brother. Here and now.

Lucky held her hand while she told the story, giving her the strength to tell the whole thing.

"I want Ava to stay here. She's safer. They almost got her this morning because we didn't see them coming. That won't happen if she's here."

"Of course, you're both welcome to stay as long as you need," said Jack.

"I don't believe it will be too long," said Lucky. "I'll be talking to Delilah shortly. I will have answers and then, I'll have bodies. No one tries to kidnap my wife or kill me without payback."

Her husband sounded a little bloodthirsty, but she didn't blame him or disagree with him. The man he was after had killed Jeffrey and nearly killed Lucky this morning. No, she wanted some payback, too.

Ava looked up at Lucky. "Do you really

think Delilah told them where to find me?"

He nodded. "I don't believe anyone else knew your secret and wanted to hurt you and I at the same time."

"I'll go with you," said Jack. "I'll have your back."

"Thanks. I'd appreciate it. There are two of them. A big one who I wounded and a regular sized man who I didn't. He kept me busy so I couldn't go after the big guy. One stick and I missed my target." His hands fisted on the table. "I need to practice. I've slacked off since I got married. I can't do that anymore."

"Don't blame me," said Ava. She placed her hand over Lucky's and squeezed. She wanted him to know she was there and supported him. "You can take whatever time you need."

She dropped her hand back to her side and looked over at Rita. "This will put a hold on opening the jewelry store. Until these men are taken care of, I won't be leaving this house. I know what they are capable of."

Ava's gaze went from Lucky to Jack and back again. "Don't let them cut you. Their knives are poisonous. That's what killed

Jeffrey, the poison, not the wound."

"I'm relieved to hear you don't want me killed," said Lucky.

"Of course, I don't want you dead, you big lummox."

She laid her hand on Lucky's arm. "You're the father of my baby. I intend for you to help me raise him…or her."

She watched Lucky's face and for a moment she thought he was disappointed that she hadn't said she loved him and that's why she didn't want him dead. Of course, she did love him, and she wanted to tell him, but was afraid to put her heart out there to be broken again.

"When will you see Delilah?"

Lucky stood.

"I'm going there now. Sam Jones at the Longbranch gave her a job. You'll be safe. Don't go into town until I come back. I'll have more information then."

"All right. Be safe."

Lucky pulled her to her feet and kissed her hard. When he broke the kiss he smiled.

"You won't forget me now," said Lucky.

Forget him! Her pulse raced and standing up, rather than collapsing onto her chair, took every last bit of effort. Her lips tingled and she was sure they were swollen.

"I appreciate the kiss, but I wouldn't have forgotten you without it. You're a pretty unforgettable man."

He grinned.

"I intend to stay that way."

He stepped away and glanced at Jack.

"You ready?"

"Wouldn't miss it for the world," answered Jack.

Jack looked at Rita and placed his hand on hers where it rested on the table.

"Get your gun and keep it handy."

"Thought I would."

"Rita has a gun?"

Ava looked over at Lucky.

"I want to learn how to shoot."

"After this is taken care of, maybe Jack will teach you. He's much better with his pistol than I am."

Ava turned toward Jack.

"When everything is over and behind us, will you teach me?"

"You won't have much reason to learn after this."

She stood straighter. "But I will. I'll have Rita, and she'll have me to protect when we go into business together."

"That's a good point. I think you should have a guard on duty at all times," said Jack.

"That's a good idea," said Lucky. "We'll discuss it when Jack and I get back."

"We'll talk about anything you want, just come home safe," said Ava. Her stomach was in knots and she was sure that the baby had nothing to do with them.

He kissed her again.

Not hard, not fierce, but gentle and loving.

He pulled back and ran a finger down the side of her face.

"We'll talk about a lot of things when I get back."

What does that mean? Will he finally tell me he loves me? Will we talk about the jewelry store, the baby, the gems...love? I want him to build us a house is that what he wants to discuss? What in the heck does he want to talk about?

Ava was frustrated, anxious and had morning sickness. She'd been shot at and almost kidnapped. So far the day was not starting at all well.

*****

Emmett Walsh's hotel room
Old Miner's Inn

"Carl. Carl. We need to get you to a doctor. The knife wound is bad. You'd be dead now if the man's aim had been better."

Carl opened his eyes. He sat on the bed, his back to the wall and his right hand pressing a towel against his wound.

"I'm here. What makes you think he could throw that knife any better than he did?"

"You were holding his wife and he threw the blade anyway. It is clearly his weapon of choice, though he was not bad with the pistol either."

"If the doctor can sew me up, I'll be all right. But I won't be able to help you with any knife work, my arm is too weak. So poison is out for this one."

"That's all right. I'll carry poison on my blade. I may not be as good as you but I can handle a knife in a pinch. Delilah told me where Madigan will take Ava, and it will be difficult, but not impossible. We will have to come through the forest on the back side of the house."

"Where is that?"

"To his friend. Jack Colton."

"If these jewels were not worth so much money, I would say to forget it and consider ourselves lucky to still be alive."

"Ah, but my dear Carl, they are worth so much. Several million dollars. That makes all this, including your wound, worth the effort. For now, let us go find a doctor to sew you up."

Walsh put Carl's jacket around his shoulders.

They left the inn and found a doctor willing to stitch the knife wound closed. He also put Carl in a sling so he wouldn't move his right arm and rip out the stitches. But above all else the doctor was not the same one who sewed up Delilah. He was a man who knew how to keep his mouth closed.

*****

Lucky and Jack arrived at the Longbranch saloon just in time to see a doctor run inside before them. They parked the carriage in front.

"What do you want to bet he's here for Delilah?" asked Lucky.

"Even I wouldn't take that bet."

They made their way through the throng of people until they were finally in her room. Delilah was bruised and battered. Everything on the left side of her face was turning color. Someone had taken out their frustrations on her. Both of her eyes were blackening and her jaw on the left side was swollen. The doctor didn't want her talking and shortly she wouldn't be able to.

Lucky didn't see any knife or gunshot wounds, so hopefully she would make a full recovery.

"Lucky."

His name was a mere whisper from her lips.

"Lucky."

"I'm here Dee. I'm here."

"He wants her bad. Ava."

"Is it Walsh? Emmett Walsh?"

"Yes."

"Did he do this to you?"

"Yes. He...he...enjoyed beating me up."

"I won't let him hurt her. Don't worry."

"I was wrong. Keep her safe."

"That's enough talking, young lady," said Doctor Goad. "I'm wrapping your jaw shut. I don't want you talking."

The doctor looked at Jack and Lucky.

"No talking at all," insisted Doc.

"I have just one last question for her doctor. Please," said Lucky.

"All right one," conceded the doctor.

"Is Walsh the big guy or the small one?"

asked Lucky.

"Small," whispered Delilah.

"Enough," said Doc. "I want her taken back to my office where I can watch over her."

The doctor moved a short distance away from Delilah and motioned for Lucky to follow.

"I think she'll heal from this but I don't know about her voice, whether she'll be able to sing or not. Sometimes victims of strangling attempts regain all of their voices, sometimes they won't. It all depends on what she thinks she has waiting for her when she's better. Do you understand, son?"

Poor Delilah. She may never sing again. I'm so sorry for her.

"I understand, Doc, but I can't be what she wants me to be. I'm married now. I'll try to help her if I need to, but I'm sure that the owner of the Longbranch will see that she's taken care of."

"Just so long as we understand each other."

"We do."

"Will your wife object?"

His brows furrowed for a moment. "I believe my wife would be the first one to lend a helping hand. She's gentle that way. I'm giving my word on this."

"Glad to hear it. We need more people like that. Now I'll escort her to my office."

Lucky watched as two men lifted Delilah on a stretcher and carried her out of the saloon. He looked around to see if anyone was watching with particular interest and saw one man. A dandy in a gray suit with graying brown hair and a thin moustache. Why did he stick around and risk being seen? Lucky didn't know unless perhaps he thought this would draw Ava out.

The man saw Lucky watching him and tipped his head.

The 'catch me if you can' gesture made Lucky's blood pound. He'd take the man and show him what it's like to be beat nearly to death.

A hand on his shoulder told him Jack was at his back.

"Let's get back to our wives. Nothing more we can do here."

"You're right. Thank you for letting us stay with you. I need to build Ava a house. This has shown me just how important a home is, especially if you are having kids." *Maybe I should build a small cabin for us to stay in until the ground is warm enough to be able to dig a foundation.*

Jack clapped Lucky on the back.

"You can't do anything about the house for another four or five months. The ground is too hard for a good foundation. But we can, and will, do something about this situation much, much sooner than that. Do you think he'll make a try for her at our house?"

Lucky led the way out of the saloon and toward the carriage. "He's got to. He wants those stones and the only way he can get them is through her."

Jack frowned. "Are you telling her we're using her as bait?"

Lucky got into the carriage after searching the area around them for Emmet Walsh and not seeing him.

"No. Did you tell Rita when you used her?"

Jack climbed in and took up the reins.

"Giddy up!"

He cracked the whip over the horses heads and they began to trot.

"Of course not. Do I look stupid?"

"Nope. Do I?"

"Only if you haven't told her you love

her, yet."

"You know how I feel about love. Nothing good can come of it." *I don't love her. I'm incapable of loving a woman but if I could, then Ava is the woman I would love.*

"You're wrong, Lucky. Only good comes from real love. If you'd let yourself, you'd discover that you already love Ava. I can see all the signs that I had and wouldn't believe. You remember telling me what a fool I was for refusing to believe that I loved Rita? The same is happening with you."

"You know what Tess did to me. I can't be put in that position again."

"You're not. You're already married to Ava, twice. You and Tess were only engaged. The fact that she didn't want to wait and married your brother instead doesn't reflect on you or your feelings. She was a pig."

Lucky looked sharply at Jack and saw a smile on his face. Lucky threw back his head and laughed.

*****

Ava read while Rita knitted as they sat in the parlor awaiting their husbands' return.

Ava put down her book, curiosity getting the better of her.

"Rita, why did Jack teach you how to shoot a gun?"

"Gangsters were trying to kill me. I witnessed a murder by one of the Whyos gang."

Ava shuddered. "I've heard of them. An Irish gang, aren't they?"

"The murderer didn't know I was in the alley on the side of a burlesque house. I never actually saw his face until he came to Central City. Long story short, he came after me here and ended up dead. Jack had to kill him. He didn't give Jack any choice."

Our situations are similar in that someone was after her, but they wanted her dead.

"Oh, my gosh. Weren't you scared?"

"Terrified and yet, I hated the way that Jack and the boys—"

"The boys?"

Rita smiled and blushed.

"That's what I call Lucky, Robert and Henry. The boys. Anyway, they wanted to keep me locked up here, all safe and sound. All I felt was that I was in prison. A gilded cage is beautiful, but it is still a cage."

"I understand that, but this man is too dangerous. I'd rather be here than out there even though the man after me doesn't want me dead necessarily he just wants the jewels that Jeffrey gave me."

"But he'll kill you to get them,"

"Yes. He killed Jeffrey with poison on the blade of a knife. I'm terrified the same thing could happen to Lucky."

"How long have you been in love with him?"

"I'm not." She lifted her chin and crossed her arms over her chest as though that would protect her heart. *I can't admit that I love him and yet having someone to talk to about it would be nice.*

Rita lowered her chin, raised an eyebrow and looked at Ava through her lashes.

"Don't look at me like that. I refuse to love him. He doesn't love me and I won't risk my heart..." She took a deep breath. "Does it show so much?"

"Only to another woman who has been in that position."

Ava's eyes welled with tears.

"He says love makes men do stupid things, and he won't be stupid about anything."

"Men do stupid things without being in love. Like kill people. If Danvers hadn't killed Mulligan, then Danvers wouldn't have come here looking for me and lost his life in the process. Stupid."

"I suppose you're right. I don't like thinking that Jeffrey did something that caused his death. But he insisted he's the one who found the jewels in the Incan tomb and he had the document with the Peruvian government that he gave me. Emmett Walsh has no claim on these gems."

Rita put her knitting in the basket on the floor beside the chair and stood.

"Come on to the kitchen, let's get a cup of tea and some cookies. I make great gingerbread cookies and tea cakes, they are a soft, thick sugar cookie. You'll love them."

Ava put her book down and stood, stretched and followed Rita.

"Sounds wonderful. Maybe then I won't worry so much about Lucky and Jack. I wish they'd hurry home with good news."

CHAPTER 10

The men returned and joined Rita and Ava in the kitchen. The news wasn't good. Delilah had been beaten nearly to death and Lucky had promised to help the woman get back on her feet.

That was fine, all Ava had to do was remember that Lucky married her, twice, of his own free will. He could have married Delilah if he wanted, but he didn't. The first time he wed Ava, he was keeping the bargain and the second time was because she was pregnant. What if she wasn't pregnant? Not much likelihood of that considering the morning sickness.

"Rita can you show us to our room, please?" She looked up at Lucky. "Are you ready to check out our room for the foreseeable future?"

"I am."

He put his arm around her waist and brought her close.

"I'm ready for anything that gives me a

reason to be alone with you," he whispered.

Ava swatted his chest.

"Oh, you. Be good."

He chuckled.

"I'm sure you're probably exhausted," said Rita. She was ignoring Lucky's antics or hadn't heard. "I find that I'm still tired and I thought my energy level would be better after the first trimester."

"Trimester? What is that?" *I have a lot to learn if I don't even know the vocabulary.*

"The doctor says that pregnancy is divided into three periods of three months each called trimesters. In the first trimester is the morning sickness, so far the second has me plagued with fatigue. Heaven knows what the third trimester will bring."

Rita led the way up the stairs.

"I hope you don't mind but I put you farthest away from us. I thought we could each use the extra privacy."

Ava shook her head. "We don't mind at all, do we dear?"

"No. Not at all,"

"I call the room the blue room because the drapes, wall paper, carpets and so forth are blue. I hope you like it."

She opened the door and ushered Ava

and Lucky inside.

"Why, it's lovely," said Ava. "For some reason I thought the decor would be overwhelming with all the blue, but it's not."

"I just want to thank you for having us here at all," said Lucky as he swept his hand to indicate the space.

"Why, of course. You two are always welcome here," said Rita.

"This is only temporary, just until we can eliminate the threat to Ava."

"Yes. Then we get to return to the apartment above the saloon."

Ava heard the sarcasm in her voice but she didn't care.

"Yes, well, ah, I'll leave you to get settled."

Rita left the room.

Lucky turned to Ava.

"That wasn't very subtle."

"Subtle? My words were as restrained as I get concerning our living conditions. I want a house, now more than ever."

"Because you're expecting?"

"That, and the fact I'd feel safer. We wouldn't have hundreds of people traipsing through the lower floor of our home every day."

He walked over and wrapped his arms around her.

"I promise to build us a house just as soon as the weather allows."

A burst of joy filled her chest. "Really and how long is that? Will the baby be here already?"

"That depends. When do you think the baby is due?"

She paused to calculate the date. "Probably July or August."

"We'll have the house built by then unless you want a really huge one in which case it will take a little longer."

"I don't need a big house, just one with six bedrooms for us and for the kids, one for the housekeeper and one for the cook."

"Five bedrooms for kids?"

Lucky swallowed hard and rubbed the back of his neck.

"Are you sure? That's a lot of children."

Ava grinned and put her arms around his waist. "That was sarcasm. Yes, I want a huge house. I want lots of children. I don't plan on having them all at once. Growing up there was just me and Jeffrey. When he wasn't around I was...lonely. I don't want our children to ever feel that way. There is a difference between being alone and being lonely."

He placed his arms around her.

"I know. A person can be lonely in a room full of people."

"Exactly."

Lucky looked around the room.

"Rita left. Do you want to break in the bed?"

He waggled his eyebrows.

Ava couldn't help but giggle. He had a way of making her feel like a girl with no cares in the world.

"They'll know. It's the middle of the day."

He grinned.

"Of course, they'll know. They put us at this end of the house for a reason. They'll probably be doing the same thing."

She started unbuttoning the bodice of her dress.

"No time for that, sweetheart. This one is hard and fast. Drop your bloomers and lie across the bed with your legs hanging down the side."

Titillated by his odd request, she did as he said.

"That's right. Now let me make love to you."

She wanted to tell him it wasn't love, just sex, but she also wanted him too much to disagree.

A short while later, he was collapsed on top of her, both of them were sated and breathing hard.

He kissed her soundly.

"You are magnificent."

"You're not too bad yourself."

He kissed her again and then stood to right his clothing.

Ava put on her bloomers, tied the tapes at her waist, dropped her skirt and smoothed it with her hands to remove any wrinkles.

"Shall we go and present ourselves to our hosts?"

He held his arm out toward her.

"We shall."

*****

Since she'd told them about the jewels and Jack had a safe they could be put in, Ava brought the pouches downstairs that night after dinner. She poured the bags out into the middle of the card table in Jack's office.

"My God, Ava. No wonder this man it

after you. There are hundreds of gems here. Millions of dollars," said Jack.

"I know, but they're mine and I'm not giving them up to the man who killed Jeffrey. That is just not happening."

"I'm not saying you should," said Lucky. "But I'm glad we're here so Jack can put them in his safe."

"I've never see so much sparkle in my life," said Rita.

She picked up one of the bigger stones, a sapphire. "Look at the deep blue color. It's almost the violet of your eyes, Ava."

"I know and others are quite pale." Ava plucked one of the light blue stones from the mound of jewels and held it so she could see the lamp light behind it. "So much so I believe they are blue diamonds not sapphires."

"And these other stones?" asked Jack, fingering a light green gem.

"That's an emerald, even though it's so light. Emeralds run the gamut of pale grass green to the dark green you're probably used to seeing. The light ones are actually the more valuable because they are rarer." She pulled a couple the stones aside each time she named a new stone. "Rubies, white diamonds, blue diamonds, yellow diamonds, sapphires, black diamonds and one large pink diamond."

She pulled the stone, the size of an egg toward her.

"Look at this."

She took out a jeweler's loupe, handed it and the stone to Lucky.

"Tell me what you see."

He put the instrument to his eye and examined the diamond.

"I don't see anything, just the pink stone."

"You don't see any lines or cracks or dark spots?"

"No, just pink stone."

Ava grinned, nearly bouncing in her chair. She hadn't felt this excited since she'd looked at her first flawless diamond.

"Exactly. That stone alone is worth a million dollars because it is so large and flawless. I can't wait to set it off in a magnificent gold setting. I just don't know if I should make it a necklace or a tiara."

"A necklace would be much easier to sell," said Rita.

"That's true," said Ava.

She looked around at all of them, her

husband and her friends. Each held a stone and they were passing the loupe between them to look deeply at the jewels.

"I don't know if it means anything," said Jack. "But every piece I've looked at is…perfect."

"I think you'll find that they are all that way. I've not been able to look at every stone yet, but I'd be surprised to find any with flaws. This is the most amazing collection of stones I've ever seen," said Ava.

"We should put them away in Jack's safe," said Lucky.

"You're right. They are mesmerizing to look at though aren't they?" asked Ava.

"I never thought I would enjoy having jewels like this, but just seeing them, I want one. Jack, can we have Ava make me a ring? Please?"

Ava smiled.

"Pick any of the smaller stones. The large ones are too big for a ring on your tiny hands. I will make it as my gift for my friend."

"Oh, Ava!"

Rita leapt from the chair, ran around the table to Ava and wrapped her friend in her arms.

"You are so sweet. Thank you."

Jack eyes narrowed and his brows furrowed.

"You don't have to do that. I can pay for whatever the cost."

"Oh, the ring will be from you and me. Rita and I made an agreement, which you have to approve, but you'd provide the gold for half the earnings." She put her hand out for Jack to shake.

Jack smiled and shook Ava's hand. "All right. That works for me. What color stone would you like?"

"Anything except emerald. The emerald is a soft stone as far as gems go and doesn't make for a very good ring." Ava was happy she got to display her professional knowledge. "They are easily cracked and chipped. I would go with a diamond or a sapphire. See those pinky-purple stones? Those are called pink spinals. They are a form of sapphire and make wonderful rings."

"Actually, I was looking at this blue diamond. Is it too big?" asked Rita.

Ava looked at the stone in Rita's palm. It was about the size of the nail on her ring finger, or a pea. The stone would look spectacular on Rita's dainty hand.

"That is perfect," said Ava. "I couldn't have chosen a better stone myself. The blue diamond it will be. Jack, set aside that stone in an envelope when you put the rest away in the safe, please. We don't want to mix it with the other stones. Now, I think we should play a game of cards until bedtime. What will it be boys? Bridge or poker?" Ava picked up a deck of cards from the table, took them out of their box and expertly shuffled them.

Lucky raised his eyebrows. "You didn't tell me you play poker."

"You didn't ask." Ava was pleased she could surprise her husband. "But now that you are, Jeffrey taught me so we'd have a game to play besides gin."

"Poker is my favorite," said Rita. "I must know if Ava is any good. We might have to form our own club for ladies to play poker."

"The heck we will," said Ava. "We can take the men's money just as easily; let's not limit it to ladies."

Rita laughed. "That's exactly what I did when I first arrived. They, graciously, allowed me to sit in on their weekly game and I beat all of them, including Lucky, although, the luck of the draw was what beat him. Nothing to do with skill. Though I think he's changed his mind about me and poker."

"Ready to play gentlemen?"

Lucky grinned.

Jack cocked a dark eyebrow.

"How is it that both of our brides know how to play poker? I'm beginning to wonder about Matchmaker & Co."

Rita leaned over and patted Jack's hand.

"Come now, darling, you wouldn't have it any other way. Ava can be the sixth on poker nights, at least until Robert and Henry get married. Then we'll need a bigger table."

"But they may not know how to play poker," said Lucky.

"Then we'll teach them," said Rita.

"Looks like you better invest in a bigger table, Jack," said Lucky. "Our ladies are determined to join us."

Guilt stabbed Ava's thoughts.

"I'm sorry. We shouldn't force ourselves on you during your poker games. So when you are having your men's night, the ladies will come to our house, which hopefully will be finished by then, and we'll play our own games."

"We don't mind playing with you ladies. Truly, I find it quite entertaining," said Lucky as he put his hand on Ava's.

"As do I," said Jack. He leaned over and kissed Rita.

Lucky sat back in his chair and stared at Ava.

"Some day you and I are having our own game of poker. A special game not fit for card rooms."

She sat straighter in her chair. "I'll still beat your pants off."

Lucky cocked an eyebrow. "Oh, I'm hoping that you do, my dear. Hoping that you do."

After a few moments Ava understood and immediately felt the heat in her cheeks.

"Lucky! Behave yourself."

Jack started laughing.

Lucky roared with laughter.

Even Rita giggled behind her hand.

"Laugh all you want, husband. I will get even," said Ava, though she was smiling.

"I'll be waiting, wife," replied her husband with a lethal grin.

"Get the chips. Let's play," said Rita.

Amid all the frivolity Ava was ever aware that out there in Central City tonight, was a murderer and he was determined to get her gems, no matter what obstacle she put in front of him, even herself.

CHAPTER 11

Ten days after being knifed Carl went back to see the doctor and had the stitches removed.

"There Carl. How do you feel now?" asked Emmett.

"I feel like breaking some heads."

"Good, you're back to normal."

Emmett turned to the doctor.

"Thank you, Doctor. You've been very helpful and have proven you can be trusted. Had it been otherwise you would be dead now. As it is, you get to live."

The doctor began to sweat. He took his handkerchief from his pocket and mopped his forehead.

"Th...th...thanks, mister. I don't want to know anything more than that. The doctor pointed at Walsh. "You're mister and he's Carl, and I ain't never seen you."

"Good. Good. Farewell, Doctor."

Emmett turned away and then turned back. He reached in his pocket and pulled out a double eagle gold coin.

"For your time and your silence. I'll know if you talk to anyone."

The doctor raised his eyebrows a little and gave a single shake of his head. "About what?"

"That's right. Let's go, Carl."

Carl opened the door for Emmett, and they walked out of the doctor's office.

"Now we need to find out more about the Colton house," said Emmett.

*****

The first morning of their stay with Jack and Rita, Ava awoke with a start. She'd been dreaming of Emmett Walsh. *The person in my dream was faceless, but I know it was him. I was running from him and he was coming after me with a knife. I ran. He was closer. "Give me the jewels, Ava. You don't have to die like Jeffrey did...I'll make yours quick...*

The sky was still dark and the moon had not completely set. She figured it was about two o'clock in the morning. As was normal, Lucky's arm rested across her stomach, holding her close. She smiled, lifted his arm, scooted out from under it and then got out of the bed.

She put on her nightgown and robe before going downstairs. Hoping it was still too early for her to have morning sickness, she headed to the kitchen for a snack. She noticed a light in the parlor and went to investigate.

Ava peeked into the room and saw Rita curled up in one of the overstuffed arm chairs, reading a book. Ava knocked softly on the door.

Rita looked up from her book.

"Come in. What are you doing up so early or late as the case may be?"

"I was hungry and decided to see what you had in the icebox. And you?"

"I'm always up. When I was a dancer I didn't usually get to bed until the wee hours of the morning. I haven't completely gotten used to the idea of bedtime being so early, so I go to bed with Jack and after he falls asleep I get up and come down here to read or knit, but mostly to dance. I don't get the opportunity to dance much otherwise and I want to keep in practice."

Rita stood and stretched several different ways.

"I always stretch when I get up from reading. Let's go see what wonders Mrs.

Potts has left us in the icebox."

Ava walked with Rita to the kitchen which was located at the back of the house.

Once they arrived Rita opened the icebox and rummaged around.

Ava stood behind her and looked over her shoulders.

"There are leftovers from dinner which surprises me, usually there aren't any. Jack normally eats them before bed."

"How about just a glass of milk and some cookies? Do you have any cookies left? Those gingerbread ones you made are spectacular. Do you think I'll have morning sickness? Should I stick to dry toast and tea?"

"Hmm. I'm not sure. I think you'll be fine. I was. My sickness was literally morning sickness. I only was ill at breakfast time, but everyone is different. No way to know unless you try."

"Good morning, ladies."

Ava turned at the sound of Jack's voice and saw him standing in the doorway.

Rita looked up and smiled.

"Come in, my love. Did you miss me?"

"Always."

"So this is where everyone is at a quarter

to three in the morning in the Colton house."

Ava saw that Lucky was joining them. He looked good enough to eat dressed in his pants with his shirt unbuttoned two buttons so just a little of his chest hair showed.

He came over to Ava and gave her a quick kiss.

"I missed you," he said softly while he held her close.

"It's amazing how quickly we get used to having someone sleeping with us, isn't it?" Jack put his arms around Rita.

"It is. I never let anyone stay with me before," said Lucky.

"I didn't either. Marriage does strange things to a man," admitted Jack.

Jealousy coursed through Ava's veins. "I really don't want to hear about the women you had in your bed before me."

"Nor do I," said Rita.

"Sorry, ladies." Jack leaned over and kissed his wife's cheek. "You know I love only you."

"Yes, sorry," agreed Lucky.

Rita got four glasses and filled them with ice cold milk.

Ava took the glasses to the table and set one in front of each of the men and the place

Rita would sit. She sat next to Lucky and took a sip of the milk before she put the glass on the table. It seemed to stay down all right.

Rita brought a plate of her gingerbread cookies to the table and took a seat next to Jack.

"I love these cookies," admitted Rita. "They're my favorite."

"Mine, too, though I do love the tea cakes with a cup of coffee," said Jack.

Rita beamed.

"Thank you. I'm gratified to know that you like what I bake."

Jack patted his flat stomach.

"I like it too much."

"You won't make us feel sorry for you that you are getting such wonderful treats all the time. You lucky bas—"

"Gentlemen, please," said Rita. "No cussing."

"Even when we talk about Emmett Walsh?" asked Ava.

I want to cuss...and kick and scream at the man. She wanted him to feel her pain and then she wanted him to die.

Ava closed her eyes for a moment and shook her head, getting the scenario out of her mind. *What is the matter with me? I've never wished death on anyone in my life, but then I'd never lost Jeffrey to a murderer, either. There needs to be retribution, an eye for an eye.*

"That would be an exception," admitted Rita. "Most definitely."

Ava took a sip of milk and swallowed the bite of cookie she'd just taken.

"I'm sorry. I had a dream about him, so he was on my mind. I will not think about him. Pass me another cookie, please."

Lucky handed her the plate of gingerbread cookies.

She took one and set the plate on the table in front of her. Ava knew with the mood she was in that more cookies would be eaten this night.

After Rita and Jack regaled Ava with stories about their first few months of marriage, Ava felt better about her own difficulties. Maybe they needed to use her to bring Walsh out into the open, like they did with Rita.

"The jewels are safe here. You should go about getting that shop space. It's a great location and after Emmett Walsh has been taken care of then it's just a matter of having the equipment. You and I should see about a lease tomorrow. Ted Bishop, the owner will be here in Central City on other business. What do you say?" asked Lucky.

Ava's heart leapt. Her dream of her own shop was coming true, thanks to Jeffrey. Even in death he was taking care of her.

She nodded.

"I would like that very much. Then maybe we can go to the hardware store and have him order the equipment I need. I've put off making jewelry for so long, I'm afraid I may not remember how."

"You won't forget. Trust me. I was afraid I'd forget how to dance, too, but I remember. When I dance at night the steps come to me without effort. What do you need?" asked Rita. "I know nothing about making jewelry."

"Well, I'll need to be able to melt the gold, make molds, clean the jewelry and many other things I'm not thinking of right now."

Ava covered a yawn with her hand. She couldn't help it. Fatigue was creeping up now that they were relaxed and she stifled another yawn behind her hand.

"All right, that does it. Time for bed."

Lucky stood.

"I am tired now," admitted Ava.

Lucky took Ava's hand.

"We'll see you both in the morning."

Once out of earshot of Jack and Rita, Lucky whispered naughty things in Ava's ear and she found she wasn't nearly so tired after all.

*****

Ava dressed in a pretty soft pink frock which looked wonderful with her pale skin and sable brown hair.

Lucky came up behind her, as she stood in front of the mirror, and put his arms around her, pulling her back against him.

"You look beautiful. When will you start to show?"

He his hands settled over her stomach.

She put her hands on top of his.

"I don't know. I haven't asked Rita yet or seen the doctor. I'm sure both of them can tell me."

"You know, I think I can see a bump just starting when you're naked."

She rolled her eyes.

"You cannot. I didn't even know I was expecting and now you can see it? I think it's all in your mind."

He chuckled and kissed her neck.

She angled her head, giving him access to her sensitive skin.

"Perhaps. Maybe I'm just anxious to be a father."

"Are you?" She turned in his arms and looked up at him. "I was afraid you wouldn't be ready. We haven't been married but a couple of months and I—"

He put two fingers on her lips.

"You worry too much and it's not good for the baby."

She sighed, pleased by the concerned tone of his words.

"You're right. I have been worried."

He nodded. "For some good reason, it's true but you should talk to me about these things that bother you. Let me tell you now that I'm thrilled to be a father. It's time, before I get too old, to enjoy my children."

She looked down. "I feel the same way. I'm getting old."

He lifted her chin with his knuckle.

"You're only twenty-six and that's not old."

"My age seems old for a woman who wants to have children."

He grinned.

"Then we'll just have to keep trying to have children. The practice is more than half the fun."

She laughed. He always made her smile or laugh. Oh, he was serious when the situation called for it, but if there was a silver lining to be found, Lucky could find it. At least he did for her.

"Lucky, when will you tell me why you think love makes men foolish? You said you've watched what love does to men and you want nothing to do with it. And I know that your fiancée married your brother rather than wait."

He dropped his arms to his sides, walked over to the window, put his left hand up on the side and leaned on his arm. He put his right hand into his front pants pocket and then stared out.

Ava walked to the window and wrapped her arms around his waist. She laid her cheek against his back.

"I'm so sorry for what your brother and your fiancée did. That's horrible. But Lucky, that's not me. We're married. I'm not choosing someone over you. I chose you."

He put his hand on top of hers.

"I can't. I just can't do it. I can't say that

I'll love you when I know the situation is unlikely to happen and that I can't open myself up that much. I'm sorry, Ava. Truly I am."

She shouldn't have asked him. The tone of his voice was that of someone who is defeated. She squeezed him and then released.

"It's time to go. I want to get to see the owner before he rents the space to someone else."

Lucky turned away from the window and faced her with his hands in his pants pockets. "After we take care of that bit of business, I want to take you to see the doctor. I want him to check you, confirm you're expecting and when you're due."

She happily counted the months on her fingers. "I think I got pregnant that first week, if not the first night. That would make the baby due...mid-July. That's when she should be here. Mid-July."

He cocked an eyebrow.

"She?"

Ava nodded. "Yes. I believe we'll have a girl first and then you can have your boys."

He shook his head. "We should have the

boys first so they can look after their little sisters."

She thought of Jeffrey and how he taught her everything he knew. Ava wanted that for her daughters, too. Except she wanted more for them. She hadn't forgotten that she'd run to Lucky when Walsh came that first time in the saloon. Ava realized that she couldn't have taken on two grown men and knew when to run. Her daughters needed that knowledge, too.

"My girls will not need looking after because their father will teach them all the same things he teaches his sons. He will also teach them when to run. Facing two armed men in the kitchen is not the time to make a stand and try to fight. I know that, so I ran to you. Our daughters need that knowledge as well."

"I will teach them to able to care for themselves and when to be wary. They won't be at any man's beck and call."

"They will be independent."

"Not *too* independent though and I expect their mother to teach them about making a home for their husbands."

Their mother. I'll really be a mother. I can hardly wait. "I can do that. They will have the best from both worlds. I hope the knowledge will serve them well."

"It will. You'll see. Now are you ready to go? We'll stop and eat breakfast first."

They went down to the kitchen where Jack and Rita were having breakfast.

"Rita, we're looking at the shop today. Do you want to come with us?" asked Ava. She grabbed a plate, two pieces of dry toast and a cup of tea.

Lucky piled his plate with eggs, breakfast meats, toast and then got a cup of coffee to go with it.

Ava would love to have a cup of coffee with breakfast. She missed that more than anything, but she had to admit that the tea settled her stomach whereas the coffee did not.

Rita shook her head.

"I would but I'm feeling a little under the weather this morning. I think I'll stay in."

"I hope you feel better soon. I noticed you're having tea and dry toast. Is the food helping?" Ava looked at her friend and furrowed her brows. "Do you think it's the baby? Do you need the doctor?"

Rita smiled. "You sound like Jack. I

think I'm just tired and yes, I do think it's because of the baby. I told you that fatigue was what was plaguing me this trimester."

Ava nodded. "That's right I remember now. Since you've been in the assayer's office before, you already know what it looks like. This will be my first time, but I'm sure it will serve our purposes very well. I'm so excited to start being creative again. Working with my hands, making something beautiful…I can hardly wait."

"I think this space will be perfect for us, too," said Rita. "This will be so much fun."

"I know. See you later."

Ava finished her toast and tea, then she stood walked around to Rita and hugged her.

"I'll come see you when we get back."

Lucky held Ava's coat for her and they left though the kitchen door to go to the stable. They were borrowing Jack's buggy for the day, which Ava was glad for. The thought of walking into and around town with the chill in the air, didn't appeal to her at all.

Barney had Jack's buggy ready and waiting when they arrived.

"Here you are, Mr. Madigan."

The young man held the horses by the

bits in their mouths while Lucky helped Ava onto the seat. Then he climbed in next to her.

She covered their laps with a blanket for warmth and they headed to their appointment in town.

*****

From his perch on the mountain behind the house, Emmett saw the buggy pull away and head toward town. He and Carl could easily get into the house through the kitchen door. Carl would have to take care of the stable boy, just tie him up and put him in a stall. No killing. Not if Emmett could help it. He didn't want to be exposed to frontier justice and hanged without a trial.

Now the solution was just a matter of finding the right time to do this. The men must be out of the house, so today wasn't good. They'd travel up here every morning to find out who left and who stayed. He could handle the women, but the men would be more difficult. Men tended to fight back.

"Today is not the day, Carl. We'll have to come back tomorrow. I want those jewels, but I don't need to face two guns to get them."

Carl frowned and kicked the tree he

stood next to.

"I don't like waiting, Emmett. If I was not injured we could do it today, guns or not."

"Now Carl, waiting is fine. We'll watch, look for our time. Don't lose your temper. Do you understand the jewels are worth millions?"

"I understand."

"Good. Then we will bide our time."

CHAPTER 12

Lucky's friend and the owner of the assayer's office, Ted Bishop, showed them the building.

The assayer's office was truly the perfect place for her shop. Ava fell in love with the space immediately. When they entered the building, a counter, three quarters the width of the office was the first thing to be seen. Behind the counter was a small table and chairs so the pieces of jewelry could be shown.

The building would need some cleaning and a little loving care to repair a few things, like a hole in the roof that let moisture in but that was the only major repair needed.

"Well, what do you think?" asked Lucky.

"I love it."

"Thought so. We'll take it Ted, only I'd like to buy the building rather than rent it."

Ted Bishop was a man given to extra weight around the middle. He combed his graying brown hair over the bald spot on top. His smile was genuine as he smiled at Lucky now.

"Given our last transactions, I thought you might, so I drew up papers for both the lease and the sale."

Ava put her hand on Lucky's arm. "Buy it? You're buying the building? For me?"

"Yes. For you."

"Oh, Lucky, I don't know what to say." Tears formed in her eyes and she turned away so that he wouldn't see them.

Lucky signed the paperwork and then handed the key to Ava.

"Your new store, my dear."

Ava wrapped her arms around Lucky.

"Thank you."

He hugged her back and kissed the top of her head.

"You're welcome. There's a lot of scrubbing to do but between you and Rita, you'll get it done in no time."

"I can't wait. Let's go back to the Colton's so I can get changed. Then you can take me to the mercantile so I can get cleaning supplies."

"All right."

Lucky turned to Ted.

"Thanks. Be sure and keep me in mind if you have any properties come available that I might be interested in."

"Certainly, Lucky. You two enjoy this place. I'm glad it's not staying vacant."

Ted left.

"Now before we go anywhere," Lucky pulled Ava into his arms and kissed her soundly. "I thought we might break-in owning this building right. Wait here."

He went out to the buggy and came back carrying the blanket and a picnic basket.

"We're having a picnic? Now?" Her voice squeaked.

"Yup. A small one."

He walked into the back room, she followed him.

He shut the door behind her and locked it. After spreading the blanket on the floor he pulled a bottle of champagne and two glasses from the basket.

"You really did plan for this didn't you?"

"Since last night. I borrowed the champagne from Jack. Remind me to stop by the Golden Spike and get him a replacement. Now, however, I have other plans for us."

"I haven't had champagne in years. Not since Jeffrey..." Tears filled her eyes but she didn't let them fall. Jeffrey of all people would be the happiest to see her get her own store. "When he found out that he'd gotten the approval for the dig in Peru, we had champagne the night before he left."

"I'm sorry if the champagne makes you sad. We don't have to drink it."

"No. I'm not sad. I just miss him, that's all. I definitely want to celebrate my new store."

He took her hand and led her to the blanket.

"Sit. Please."

Lucky sat cross-legged in front of Ava and poured her a glass of champagne before pouring one for himself.

He raised his glass in toast.

"To Ava's Jewelry Shop or whatever you decide to call it."

They clinked glasses.

He sipped his champagne then set the glass on the floor off the blanket. Rising he came around to her back and took her champagne from her. Then he made her turn and lie back on the blanket.

Lucky began at her ankles and caressed

her legs with his hands while pushing up her dress until she was fully exposed.

"Naughty girl. Where are your bloomers?"

Heat rose in her cheeks.

"I was hopeful you might want to christen the shop. I wanted to be prepared."

He laughed.

"A woman after my own heart."

"Yes, I am."

He doesn't realize that I really am a woman after his heart. I want him to love me, to need me to breathe just as I need him. I believe in my heart that he loves me, but refuses to admit it or perhaps doesn't recognize the feeling. But I am most definitely...after his heart.

He opened his pants and sprang forward, fully prepared for her. And then covered her, plunging into her depths.

She saw the stars and was replete.

Lucky shouted, and then collapsed upon her.

"Why can't I get enough of you? I've never had this problem with any other woman, but you... I simply want to be with you every moment. When I'm not with you, I think about you, and when I am with you, I think about making love. What do you suppose that means?"

It means you love me you stupid man. But, I won't say that. The knowledge might scare him, and then maybe he won't separate the emotion from the act and might stop making love to me. I shouldn't care. I have my baby on the way, that is all I should care about, but it's not. I've fallen in love with him, and I want so much more.

He lay heavy upon her for only a moment before lifting himself off and righting his clothes.

She pushed down her skirt and then stood. Ava wrapped her arms around Lucky.

"Thank you for a wonderful way to christen our store."

He leaned down and kissed her. Their tongues mated neither one having to wait for the other, as they were always ready to play.

She finally pulled back.

"If we don't stop, I'll put you on your back on the blanket and christen the shop again."

He laughed.

"If you think that thought will make me stop, you're sorely mistaken, my…lady."

"All right, kind sir, shall we go back to

Jack and Rita's now? I'm anxious to get started cleaning this place but I need to change and get supplies. I don't think we'll need to go to the mercantile after all. I'm sure Mrs. Bates has everything on hand I will need."

"I'll escort you back here. Then you will lock the door and not answer it for anyone you don't know personally. Correct?"

"Correct, sir."

She saluted him.

He frowned and his eyes narrowed in anger.

"Don't."

"Don't what?"

"Salute me. That brings back memories I'd rather forget."

She laid her hand on his arm.

"I'm sorry. I won't do it again."

"Thank you."

"Of course. I would never do anything that will bring you pain."

The rest of the ride back to the Colton's was quiet. Ava snuggled up to Lucky. He put his arm around her shoulders.

They pulled up in front of the house and Ava jumped down as soon as the buggy stopped.

"You're supposed to wait until I come help you."

"I'm in a hurry and I'm perfectly capable of getting in and out of a carriage by myself."

"So I see."

"I do appreciate your help, though, when I'm not so excited. I have to get changed…" She looked over her shoulder. "I have to put on bloomers. I don't expect any additional encounters with my husband, today."

He laughed.

"I'd say you're correct about that. I'm not so uninhibited that I want to make love in front of Rita."

Ava should be scandalized but all she could do was giggle at the thought of Rita's face if she found Ava and Lucky in the throes of passion on the floor of the shop.

Ava ran up the stairs to their room and put on her old lavender dress. Now that the jewels were securely locked in Jack's safe she could wear her dress again. She found that it fit tighter than it used to. Ava put her hands on her stomach, looked up into the mirror and smoothed her dress. She still couldn't see any bulge.

Lucky entered and smiled.

"Seeing if you can make out the bump?"

She answered him without looking up.

"Yes. I can feel that I'm bigger by the way this dress fits, but I still don't see it. Don't see the baby bump."

"You will. Look again tonight when you are naked and you'll see the slight rise in your stomach where my son rests."

"Your daughter."

He grinned.

"Son. You will give me a boy, I'm sure of it."

"And I say we'll have a girl. Want to bet?"

She waggled her eyebrows.

"You know I'll beat you as I always do, so do you want to bet?"

His eyes narrowed.

"All right madam, because whichever sex the child is we will be the winners."

"That's true. So are you saying I'm right? Or are you placing your bet?"

He laughed.

"Very well, my dear. What would you like to bet?"

"I want the house to be done before the baby is born. I don't want to live above the saloon any longer. Staying here with Jack and Rita has reminded me how nice it is to live in a regular home."

"That's not something to bet on the sex of the baby. I'm building you a house just as soon as the men can break ground, but we have to wait for spring and the snow to clear."

"You know, I think the snow is beautiful to look at and it can be romantic to watch it fall while making love by the fire light, but I hate that it stops us from building right away."

"Would you like for me to see if there is a house to rent until ours is built?"

"Yes...and no. I don't want to move more than once or to buy any furniture until we are actually in the house. So I guess the answer is no. If Jack and Rita will let us, I'd rather live here until our house is built."

"So what do you bet on the baby being a girl."

"Nothing large. Just twenty dollars, because as you say, we will both be winners no matter what."

"That's true. A bet you have."

"Are you ready to go?"

"Yes, let's get the cleaning supplies and see how Rita is feeling on our way out."

They found Rita in the kitchen with Mrs. Bates. There was a wooden box on the counter and Mrs. Bates was putting things into it.

"Are you sure you're feeling up to coming to clean? You don't have to, there's plenty to do. I won't get all the cleaning done today by any means."

"No, I'm feeling much better now. I took a nap while you were gone and I feel right as rain."

"Okay, if you're sure, I appreciate the help."

Mrs. Bates put a bunch of cleaning rags on top of the supplies.

"I've given you all you need to clean and polish everything. By the time you're done the shop will sparkle. Don't forget the linseed oil," she held up the bottle. "It is for after you're done with everything else. Oil the counter and let it soak in. You can go wipe away any excess tomorrow. After that, you'll be good to go."

"Thank you, Mrs. Bates. I appreciate you sharing your knowledge with us," said Ava.

"Any time. Now," she shooed them off with waves of her hands. "Off with you all so you're back in time for supper. Mrs. Potts packed a luncheon basket for you which Barney has already put into the buggy."

"I guess that's my cue," said Lucky. "Let me get that box, ladies. Our carriage awaits."

Both woman followed Lucky outside.

*****

The following morning, Emmett and Carl were at their vigil on the hillside behind the Colton house. They watched as Ava Madigan and Rita Colton left in the buggy by themselves. This was an interesting turn of events.

"Come on Carl. We have to find out where that carriage is going.

The climbed onto their horses and followed the women.

The buggy pulled up outside a shop.

Ava pulled a key out of her reticule and opened the door.

Emmett and Carl dismounted and tied their mounts to the hitching post next to the buggy. They walked over to the shop and peered in the windows. The women were cleaning the space and looked to be staying for a while.

He looked around. The time was still

early so not many were people were around. If he was to do this, now was as good a time as any.

He and Carl tried to enter the store but the door was locked.

Emmett saw the women through the window. He watched as the Colton woman pulled a derringer from her pocket. He signaled to Carl to break the door.

The derringer went off and the bullet hit the falling door.

Emmett pulled his gun from inside his pocket and entered.

"Ladies please remain where you are. Unlike your little pistol Mrs. Colton, mine has six shots, none of which have been expended. Please put your derringer down."

He used his gun and waved the barrel toward the floor.

"Now, Mrs. Colton."

Ava never took her gaze from Walsh. "Go ahead, Rita, do as he says."

"Ava. At last we meet."

Ava started to rise.

"No quick movements. I don't want to have to shoot you when we are just getting acquainted."

She stood.

"Emmett Walsh, I presume."

"Yes. We almost met in New York, but you left before I arrived. Jeffrey did a good job of eluding us after he was wounded."

She braced her legs and pointed at him.

"You murdered him. Don't evade the truth by saying he was wounded. That makes the injury sound like he could have recovered but that was impossible wasn't it, Mr. Walsh?"

He smiled.

"Yes, you are correct. He could not possibly have recovered from the poison without the antidote, which I do carry. One never knows when one might accidently cut himself. I don't want to die because of an accident. Usually I let Carl do the knife work, but Jeffrey was a special case. I took care of him myself. However, I had no intention of sharing that cure with Jeffrey."

Ava's eyes narrowed. "You're a bastard, Mr. Walsh."

She spat the words at me. If she'd been able, she would have killed me herself for what I did to her brother.

"I am, Miss Lewis. That I am."

He smiled.

"I never knew my father."

"My name is Mrs. Madigan."

"So you married the poker player. I've done some research while we've been here, haven't I, Carl?"

"Yes, Emmett."

"Oh, ladies," he stepped to the side so they got a good look at Carl. "I forgot to introduce my associate, Carl Kroger. He is the one who will kill each of your husbands, one after the other, if you don't give me what I want."

Ava looked at Rita. Her eyes were wide and terrified.

"I don't have them here."

"I didn't believe you would, but you have Mrs. Colton and she will go get the jewels if she has any hope of seeing you alive again."

"A...Ava," said Rita.

"Just do as he says," said Ava, never taking her gaze from Walsh.

"That's right, Rita," said Walsh. "Do as I say and all will be well. Leave now, Mrs. Colton. You have exactly thirty minutes to retrieve the stones. Then I hurt Ava. Hurry Rita, hurry." He shooed her out waving his gun.

Rita looked at Ava. Ava saw her hands

shake and she was biting her bottom lip. Her friend was unsure about leaving her alone.

"I'll be fine. Just go." *I put my friend in danger, the very thing I never wanted to do. I'll do whatever he says so Rita is not hurt.*

"All right. I'm going."

Rita rushed past Walsh and Carl and out into the cold without even stopping for her coat.

Ava watched her climb in the buggy and whip the horses into a gallop. She was alone, but she had people who loved her, she refused to feel abandoned.

She turned her attention back to Walsh.

"Why are you stealing Jeffrey's stones? He found them, he paid the government their share. The rest are his...now mine. You are nothing more than a thief."

His eyes narrowed and his mouth turned down, for a moment and then he was back in control of his emotions.

"We both worked that dig. My finds were small compared to his. Some gold jewelry, a couple of crowns, even some gemstones, but Jeffrey...he found the burial chamber. He gave the agreed upon portion to the government and the rest he kept. He didn't even offer to share."

"Were you sharing your finds with him?"

He stiffened his spine. "That's neither here nor there."

"So, you weren't, and yet you expected him to share with you. You're a hypocrite as well as a bastard, Mr. Walsh."

"You can call me all the names you want, Ava. They don't bother me. I've been called worse by better people than you."

"I imagine you have. Do you mind if I sit?"

"Not at all. You have a nice little table and chairs for all of us to sit."

"I'll stand," said Carl.

"As you wish, my friend."

Ava and Walsh sat at the little table that she and Rita used for their lunch and to take breaks from the cleaning.

"He's not your friend, Carl," said Ava. "Men like Emmett Walsh don't have friends. He'll cut you out as soon as he can."

Carl's eyebrows furrowed and his eyes narrowed. "You don't know what you're talking about, so shut your mouth." He turned toward Walsh. "You wouldn't do that would you, Emmett?"

"Of course not, Carl. You and I have a

special friendship that I treasure."

Walsh pointed the gun at Ava.

"Now, please keep your mouth shut. I'd hate to have Carl gag you with his handkerchief. I doubt it's very clean."

Just the thought of being gagged with a used handkerchief made her stomach turn.

She closed her eyes, breathed deeply and opened her eyes again.

"I see that you understand my meaning."

"I do. You're disgusting."

He pulled out a pocket watch.

"You're friend has ten more minutes. I hope she makes it back here."

"She will. My friends care about me more than a bag of gems."

Ava felt a niggle of doubt, then shoved that away and knew that her friends were true.

She fisted and unfisted her hands in her skirt as she sat. For some reason the gesture eased her.

"We'll see."

CHAPTER 13

Rita pulled up in front of the house, set the brake and dropped the reins before jumping to the ground.

She ran inside. *Please let Jack be home.*

"Jack! Jack! Lucky! Lucky!"

Jack came running down the hall, followed by Lucky.

"Rita, what's wrong?"

"Emmett's got her and says he'll kill her if I don't take him the gems. Get them Jack. Now."

He didn't hesitate but ran back to his office.

"Walsh has Ava at the shop?" asked Lucky.

"Yes and I have thirty minutes to produce the jewels or he'll kill her."

"Damn." Lucky slammed his right fist into his left hand. "I should have stayed. I never should have left you all alone."

Jack slammed the safe shut.

"Here are the jewels. Let's go."

Rita moved in front of him and Lucky,

blocking the door.

"He didn't say you could come with me."

"Did he say don't bring us?"

"No, but he said he'd ki…kill you both if he didn't get the stones."

"Then we're going. Nothing will keep me from Ava, especially one little man."

"He may not be large but Carl, the man with him, is Henry's size."

Rita ran toward the front door.

"If you're coming, let's go."

Both Jack and Lucky followed Rita to the buggy. She didn't wait for them to help her in.

"Scoot over, I'm driving, Rita," said Lucky.

She was about to disagree when she looked at his face and saw the determination there, so instead she moved over.

Jack jumped into the back seat.

Lucky whipped the horses into a gallop down the driveway and didn't slow for the corner but kept them at pace. They were in front of the shop in no time. Lucky set the brake and jumped to the ground leaving Rita and Jack to their own devices.

"Walsh!" called Lucky. "I want my

wife."

Walsh came to the door of the shop with Ava in front of him, a knife at her throat.

"You don't want me to get nervous here, Madigan. I don't want to nick your wife by accident."

Lucky stopped.

"Very good. Send Rita with the jewels, then you'll get your wife."

Lucky gave the bag to Rita and she walked over to the door and handed Walsh the bag.

He gave it to Carl.

"Check and make sure it's full of gems not rocks."

Carl did as he was told.

Rita ran back to the safety of her husband behind the buggy.

"Let Ava go," called Lucky.

"No can do. I need her for insurance that you don't shoot me as soon as I leave here."

"We won't as long as you let her go," insisted Lucky. He glanced around, searching for places he could use to his advantage. If he could just get line of sight on Walsh, he'd use his knife to rid the world of the bastard.

"I can't do that...Lucky. Guess you

aren't as lucky as they say."

"You've sealed your fate," said Lucky quietly and then so Walsh could hear. "You've yet to see why I got my name."

"And I won't get to this time either. Mores-the-pity but I don't play cards. Perhaps next time."

Carl walked outside and stood as a barrier between Lucky and Emmett with his gun aimed toward Lucky.

Walsh put Ava on the horse first and then when he would have gotten quickly up behind her, her foot shot out and she knocked him away, but not far enough.

Emmett raised his gun and pointed it at Ava. "Do that again and I'll simply kill you and your husband now. Do you understand?"

She nodded.

He mounted behind her and took off toward Golden. Carl glanced at Walsh's retreating form, then back at Jack and Lucky. He turned and got on his horse and followed Walsh.

Lucky's right hand rested on his knife, while the other fisted and unfisted in frustration.

"I'll take the path by the river. The route

will save time and I can cut them off before they reach the second bend. I'll make Walsh sorry he crossed me."

"I'm coming with you." Jack turned and looked at Rita.

She reached up and caressed Jack's face.

"Go. Just be careful, and bring Ava back home."

Home.

Lucky realized he was only home with her. His throat tightened and his mouth went dry. Wherever Ava was, was home. They could be living in the saloon or a tent by the river. The location mattered not as long as his beloved wife was there, that place was home.

The three climbed into the buggy and took off toward Jack and Rita's with Lucky driving.

"Rita, have Barney saddle the roan and the appaloosa," said Jack once they arrived.

"On it."

Lucky ran up the stairs two at a time without missing a step and ran down the hall to his and Ava's room. Once there, he pulled his carpet bag from under the bed and took out his throwing knives. He slid one in each boot and another two under his belt. Then he put on his double holster gun belt. He opened each pistol and spun the cylinder to make sure each chamber was loaded. As he replaced them in their holsters, he ran from the room. While he prepared, he divested himself of emotion so he can do what he needs to. He must be cold, exact.

He and Jack met at the top of the stairs.

"Ready?"asked Jack.

"Ready." Lucky saw Jack wearing his double holster, too. He also had an extra pistol tucked into his belt. "Walsh will rue the day he decided to take her from me. You concentrate on Carl. Emmett Walsh is mine."

When they got to the stables, Barney was waiting with the horses saddled and ready to go.

Jack mounted the big roan while Lucky got the appaloosa.

The two men looked at each other, nodded and then Lucky led the way with Jack close behind.

*****

Ava thought she was doing very well considering she'd never ridden a horse before. They were riding down the road out of Blackhawk on the way to Golden City.

They had already passed the smelter and were just passing the little white church where she'd been married…twice.

Pray for me reverend.

Her hands were white knuckled where she grasped the knob on the saddle, holding on for dear life. Walsh held her fast against him with his arm around her waist.

She turned her head so Walsh would hear her over the din of the horse's hooves striking the hard packed dirt of the road.

"You'll never get away, Walsh. Lucky will come for me, and then you'll be sorry you took me."

"I'm already sorry. Just shut your trap."

She turned her head and faced forward, refusing to let the tears fall. Fear gripped her, trapping her breath in her chest. What if Lucky *didn't* come after her? Surely, he would come for his child. That thought comforted her a bit.

They rounded a large bend, with the river on the right and a cliff on the left. Ava couldn't see around the curve and neither could Walsh until it was too late for him to stop.

Lucky and Jack were on the other side of the bend, with their guns pointing at Walsh and Carl. Lucky had his pistol in his left hand and his knife in his right.

Walsh and Carl pulled up their horses short.

The next thing she knew a knife was at her side. She gasped and tried to pull her body away from the deadly weapon.

"Stop right there Madigan. This blade is poisoned—one small prick and she'll die a slow death. I'm the only one with the antidote, so just let me go and we'll be square."

"You mean let us go, right Emmett?" asked Carl.

"Of course, both of us."

Lucky ignored Carl but she noticed that Jack's weapon was trained on Carl and didn't waver.

"Let her down. Easy. No fast movements," demanded Lucky.

"Can't do it. As soon as she's gone from me you'll have no reason to let me go."

"You're right about that, but I don't have any reason to let you go now. She's just a mail-order bride. I can get another."

Ava gasped. Those were the thoughts she'd been thinking but to have them voiced out loud hurt more than she could bear. She slumped forward to hide her tears.

Walsh grabbed at her and the knife cut her arm.

"Oww," she cried out and clutched her right arm and leaned toward the injured arm. There was an immediate burning sensation where the knife cut her and she knew she would die. The knife was poisoned and she would die just like Jeffrey.

"Ava," shouted Lucky.

She watched the knife leave his right hand in a blur, but his aim was true and Walsh fell backwards off the horse.

Carl screamed.

She'd never heard that kind of sound from a man.

Ava grabbed the reins and steadied the prancing animal.

Carl shot at Jack, but his aim was off.

Jack's wasn't.

The big, blond man fell off his horse.

Lucky reached Ava and held up his arms.

She fell into his embrace. Her legs shaky.

"He cut me, Lucky. He cut me with his poisoned blade. Search his body. He's got to have the antidote on him."

"All right. Wait here."

Lucky knelt beside Walsh's body and searched every pocket but found no bottle of anything.

"Strip him," demanded Ava. Fear, close to panic rose in her. *I don't want to die.* "He's got the antidote somewhere. He said he had it in case he nicked himself."

Lucky pulled off the man's coat, then his suit coat, and shirt. Nothing. He pulled off the left boot and then the right. That's when he saw it. He turned the boot upside down and a small glass bottle with a clear liquid in it fell out into Lucky's hand.

He unscrewed the top which was a dropper top.

"We don't know if this is the poison or the antidote. We have to get you to Doc Goad. Hopefully he'll know. I can't risk giving you something that might kill you rather than cure you."

Jack approached.

"Is everyone okay over here?"

"We hope so. Walsh cut her with a poisoned blade."

"I need to see the doctor," said Ava. "I'm not feeling well."

"Let me get my horse. Stay right there,

just a minute."

"I'm not going anywhere," she said before collapsing to the ground, her legs not able to support her.

"Ava!"

"I'm okay, just get the horse."

Lucky ran to the horse and brought the appaloosa over to her. Then he lifted her into the saddle and swung up behind her.

"Sorry Jack. I'll send someone back to help you with these bodies."

Jack waved him off. "You just get her to the doctor, don't worry about me."

Lucky kicked the horse into a gallop and drove hard for the five or so miles back to town.

He stopped in front of Dr. Goad's office, slid off the horse and let her fall into his arms.

Blood pounded in his ears and his chest was tight.

"You're okay sweetheart, do you hear me? Ava, sweetheart, listen. I love you, Ava. I don't want to lose you, so don't even think about dying. You hear me? Ava? Shit!"

He hurried up the walkway as fast as he could, fumbled with the door handle and finally just kicked in the door.

"Doctor! Doctor Goad!"

"Great Scott, what is the problem," shouted the doctor.

"She was cut with a poisoned knife. I have what I think is the antidote, but I'm not sure, so we didn't give it to her."

"Follow me."

The doctor went to one of the rooms with a bed.

Lucky laid Ava on the mattress.

He straightened and dug in his shirt pocket.

"Here's the bottle we found on him."

The doctor took the bottle and opened it, sniffed, tasted and poured the entire contents into Ava's mouth.

"Let's hope this is not too late but I believe she'll pull through. These next twenty-four hours will tell the tale."

"She's expecting, Doc."

"You should be aware then that she could lose the child. I'm not sure how these chemicals will affect her pregnancy."

He felt like someone had just punched him in the gut.

"I care about *her*, Doc. I'm sorry as I can be about this child if we lose it, but we'll have other babies. I need Ava."

Doc pulled the blanket up and covered Ava. He picked up her hand and held it for a short time before gently settling her arm across her chest.

"I'll do my best. The antidote was a common one for a multitude of poisons. I don't believe the poison was anything exotic, which would be a difficult problem without the knife to try and determine the variety used."

"We still have the knife. Do you need it?"

"I may. Can you get it for me?"

"Sure. I need to help Jack get the bodies back to Sheriff Wade."

"Bodies?"

"The men who tried to take her from me. They are dead." His hand formed a fist. "No one takes Ava from me. I'll bring the knife to you. Watch her for me, Doc. I can't lose her."

*****

When Lucky got back to the site of the shooting, Jack had re-dressed Walsh and tied him onto his horse. He struggled with Carl Kroger.

The body was too big to be handled by one man alone.

"Here, let me help."

Lucky slid from his horse and ran to Jack. He picked up one of Carl's arms and Jack the other. They pulled the man to a standing position and then leaned his arms over the saddle. Grabbing a leg each man lifted until Carl lay across the horse's saddle on his belly.

Lucky held him in place while Jack tied his hands to his ankles underneath the horse's stomach. No way was Carl's body falling off.

Lucky turned toward Jack.

"Where's the knife? Walsh's knife?" He glanced around the ground.

"In the sheath on his belt. Why?"

"The doctor thinks he can determine what kind of poison is on the blade. Don't know how he'll do that, but he wanted the knife."

"I'd take it in the sheath if I were you."

"Planned on it."

He unbuckled Walsh's belt and slid off the knife. He left the belt hanging.

"Can you handle these two by yourself?"

Jack frowned and cocked an eyebrow.

"I'm letting that question pass. I know you're worried about Ava. Oh, here."

He threw a large leather pouch at Lucky.

"Here are Ava's gems. She has to get well so she and Rita can go into business. You tell her that. She can't disappoint my wife."

Lucky caught the bag and stuffed it inside his coat pocket. He had his hands on the saddle ready to mount, when he closed his eyes and blew out a breath.

"The doctor said she'll probably lose the baby. She'll be devastated."

Jack walked over and clapped Lucky on the back.

"I'm sorry. I know you were looking forward to this baby, too."

Lucky stared into the distance. "I don't want to see her so hurt. What am I to do? How do I help her?"

"You fell in love with her, didn't you? As much as you protested you wouldn't be hurt again, like Tess hurt you, for all the tea in China. So...do I start buying my tea from you?"

Lucky rolled his eyes at his friend's attempt at humor.

"I realized Ava was right. She wouldn't hurt me. Not like Tess. I just hope it's not too late. If she loses the baby, she might not want to stay. I need to make her fall in love with me."

Shaking his head, Jack started laughing.

Lucky frowned.

"What's so funny?"

"Don't you remember what you told me not that many months ago? She's already in love with you."

"She is. Well, I'll be."

Jack brows lowered over his eyes.

"Don't wait to tell her or she'll think you're saying it only because of the baby, or some other nonsense. Tell her now."

"I will. Just as soon as she wakes up."

Jack shook his head. "Say the words while she's unconscious. Maybe she can hear you."

Determination fueled his movements and Lucky swung back up into the saddle. He looked down at Jack.

"Thanks for…everything."

Jack nodded.

"You're welcome. Now go."

Lucky turned the horse toward Central City and hoped that his wife would forgive him for being such a fool. But more than anything, he wanted the woman he loved to live.

CHAPTER 14

Lucky arrived at the doctor's office with the knife in record time. The poor appaloosa was worn out. He'd have to make sure that Barney gave the animal extra grain tonight.

He walked into Ava's room to find her still unconscious with the doctor watching her.

"Has there been any change?"

"No. The antidote will take some time to work." The doctor stood and extended a hand. "Did you get the blade?"

"Yes."

He handed the doctor the knife in its sheath.

"Good. I don't know if I can discern the type of poison used. My guess would be snake venom, but she's not responding to the antidote like I would expect if it was snake."

"I'd like to stay with her, Doc." Seeing his Ava inactive brought a lump to his throat. He had to believe the doctor was right and she would recover.

The doctor nodded.

"Understandable. I'll bring in a rocking chair, it will be more comfortable. You'll have to come get me if she does anything during the night. I cleaned the wound but didn't stitch it up. I want it to drain but there was plenty of time for the toxin to get into her system."

"Doc, I…" *How do I ask if my baby is gone?* "Do you still think she'll lose the baby?"

"I don't know, but I'm not optimistic. You shouldn't be either. I don't want you to be devastated when it happens. She will be and you need to be there for her."

"I'll be whatever she needs me to be."

"Good. I'll check in again later."

Lucky nodded and picked up Ava's hand…so small and delicate in his large one, but she held his heart in her dainty hands.

She thrashed about and then was still.

He sat back in the rocking chair and watched his love fight for her life.

Something awakened him. Lucky blinked and rubbed the sleep from his eyes.

"Water."

The sound was just a whisper, but to him

the single word might as well have been a shout.

He went to the cabinet where a pitcher of water and several glasses sat. He picked up one and filled it about half-way.

Back at her bedside, Lucky slid his hand behind her head and lifted her so she could drink.

She gulped at the clear liquid until it was gone.

"More."

"In a moment, sweetheart." He hated denying her. "I have to get the doctor."

Suddenly, Ava cried out in obvious pain. She folded herself into a fetal position and cried.

"Ava! I'll be right back."

He ran to the door that connected the house to the clinic. Lucky pounded on the door.

The doctor answered quickly. He was still dressed.

"She's awake and in great pain."

"All right I'll be there in a few minutes."

"She was very thirsty. She downed the half glass I gave her without stopping to breathe. Should I give her more?"

"Yes, water is all right, but nothing else

until I examine her."

"See you shortly."

Lucky returned to Ava. She was still on her side facing the door, whimpering.

"Ava. The doctor is coming. He'll be here in a few minutes." She nodded as though she understood, but didn't stop crying.

The doctor entered the room carrying his bag.

"Ava, I need to examine you."

She shook her head violently.

"Dear, I need to see if you're losing your baby."

Ava stopped shaking her head and cried harder.

The doctor straightened her legs and lifted her dress.

"Everything will be all right. You are losing your baby Ava. I've handled this situation before and I'm sorry as I can be but I need to get the bleeding to stop. All right?"

Ava nodded. She stared at Lucky.

The look in her eyes was sad and hollow.

Lucky pushed her hair behind her ear.

"I'm so sorry," he felt his eyes fill with tears. "We'll have other babies. The most important thing is to get you well."

He reached for her hand and took it in his.

She pulled it out and looked at the ceiling.

Lucky looked up at the doctor bewildered as to what to do.

"Doctor?"

Dr. Goad raised his shoulders.

"Coming to terms with the situation will take time. Be patient."

Lucky felt helpless. He stood by her side while the doctor worked on her not knowing what else he could do.

Finally Doctor Goad moved away and washed his hands in the basin. Then he came back and talked to her.

"Ava, a small amount of bleeding is normal, but that is just from the procedure. You'll be fine. I want you to remain here for the rest of the night and then go back home with Lucky. You should stop bleeding in about a week. If you haven't or the flow gets worse, you high-tail it back here as quickly as you can. Understand?"

Ava nodded as tears leaked from the corners of her eyes.

"Tell me you understand," he insisted,

leaning over to catch her gaze.

"Yes. I understand."

Dr. Goad pulled Lucky away.

"Watch her. She's very vulnerable right now and is not thinking clearly. She will be angry with you and that is normal. Just don't let her anger get you down. Let her get the rage out. She's liable to be so upset she'll resent you. Just be prepared."

She's right to resent me. I didn't protect her. This is my fault.

"I'll do my best. That's all I can promise."

*****

The next morning Lucky collected Ava in the buggy and drove her to Jack and Rita's home.

Ava sat up straight with her hands clasped in her lap. She didn't say a word.

Nothing.

He expected something, yelling or raging anger, but the silence wasn't something he was prepared to endure.

"Ava, we need to talk."

"Why? Now you're free."

"I don't want to be free. I love you, Ava."

She started to cry. Then she looked up at

him.

"How can you be so cruel as to tell me now what I've wanted to hear for so long? I just lost my child and you think you can play games with my feelings? I don't want your pity." She slumped her shoulders. "I want a divorce."

"No. I won't give you a divorce." He fought back the tears that threatened to fall and let his anger reign free, his spine stiff. "And I don't pity you. I lost that baby, too. Do you think you're the only one grieving? Well, you're not. I wanted that child just as much as you did. I loved that child just as much as you did."

He pulled the buggy up to the Colton's front door.

When she started to get out on her own, he gripped her arm.

"We will not bring Jack and Rita into this. As far as they are concerned we are grieving together. When we are in private you can rail at me and call me names or whatever you need to do. Do you understand?"

She wrenched her arm free.

"Yes, I understand."

*****

Why is Lucky being so mean? He knows what I've been through. How can he say he loves me now? How can he play with my feelings like this?

"Ava." Rita called from the door then rushed out to the buggy. "Should you be walking? Lucky don't let her walk up to your room."

"My thoughts exactly."

He scooped Ava into his arms. She stiffened and only put her arm around his neck for stability.

Rita ran ahead of them.

"Here I'll get the doors for you."

After enduring his embrace, she saw the door to their room. The place where she could curl up in a little ball and let her sadness overtake her.

Lucky gently placed Ava on the bed.

What kind of game is this? Why is he being so caring?

"Thank you," she said softly.

"You're welcome," he whispered trailing a hand along her arm.

Rita stood with her hands clasped in front of her.

"I'll leave you two alone. Dinner and supper are at the regular times. If you'd like a tray, that's fine, too. One can be prepared for you."

"I'll make sure she is downstairs for meals," said Lucky.

She scowled.

"You can't be carrying me everywhere."

"Why not? I'm your husband. If anyone should be carrying you, it's me. Besides I get the chance to show off." He flexed his bicep.

"You're being ridiculous."

He just grinned.

He seems genuinely happy to carry me to meals. He's being so kind and he still insists he loves me. I can't believe it, not after him telling me he never would. I had accepted we would not have a marriage built on love, why can't I accept this?

The first night she was 'home' she wanted to tell him he could sleep on the couch, but no couch was in their room. She had to accept the fact of being in the bed together but that didn't mean she couldn't stay on her side and he on his.

"I don't like this, Lucky. Just because we have to sleep together doesn't mean that I feel any different or that I believe you."

"Ava, I love you and I'll do whatever I

have to so you'll believe that."

She crossed her arms over her chest. "Hmpft."

Ava walked into the dressing room and changed into a nightgown. She noticed extra pillows on a shelf and grabbed them.

"These will ensure that you stay on your side and I stay on mine."

"Pillows?"

"See?"

She placed the pillows end-to-end in the middle of the bed.

"What do you think?"

"This is silly, but I'm willing to agree to anything to appease you until you believe me when I say I love you. Don't I treat you well? Aren't I gentle?"

She stood next to the bed holding a pillow to her as though it was a shield.

"Yes, but you always have been, even when you professed to never love me. You were kind, gentle and, yes, loving then, too. What is the difference?"

He stood on his side of the bed. "I didn't realize then that I loved you. After Tess, I didn't believe feeling that emotion was possible. I'd closed myself off from the possibility. But you changed all that."

She shook her head and turned down the covers on the bed before slipping under them.

"You don't just decide overnight you love someone."

"Loving you wasn't overnight. The feeling has been building since you came, but not until I nearly lost you did I realize you were right. You could never hurt me like Tess did. You and I are already married."

He squinted his eyes and glared.

"And no divorce. One of these days you'll forgive me, until then, I'll be here for you in whatever way you need me to be. Whether that means carrying you to dinner, or helping set up your shop. You do still want to open the shop, do you not?"

With jerky moves, Lucky stripped completely.

"Put some clothes on, would you."

"No. I like that you look at me."

"Well, I don't. Looking at you makes me forget I'm mad at you."

"Good. Why don't you just admit that you love me and we can go on with our marriage like it's supposed to be? You loving me and me loving you."

Her gut wrenched and she shut her eyes for a moment. "Because it's not that easy. Don't you understand? Everything has changed. My baby—"

His hands fisted. "*Our* baby."

There was no laughter in his voice now only grief. She could hear it.

"You truly are grieving aren't you?"

He closed his eyes and clenched his jaw. When he opened his eyes they were filled with fury.

"I didn't think you cared."

"What kind of monster do you think I am, that I wouldn't care about losing my own child? Did you not hear me when we were talking about our children?"

He paced beside the bed, uncaring that he was naked.

"Did you not understand that I want many children and that each one is special to me? What do I have to do to convince you?"

He dressed. "I'm going out."

Alarm filled her. "When will you be back?"

"I don't know. Why should you care? You want a divorce, remember?"

He dressed and left the room slamming the door behind him.

Dear God. Pain stabbed her heart. What was the matter with her? Was she so selfish that she didn't believe that he grieved losing their child as much as she did? The answer was yes. She was that selfish. She thought only of herself whereas Lucky was caring for her and grieving at the same time. *She* was the monster.

Ava turned on her side and cried. Cried for herself, for Lucky and for the baby they would never hold.

Later that night she awoke to two strong arms holding her.

"Lucky?"

"Shh. Just let me hold you. We'll work our way through this. Go back to sleep." He stroked her arm.

The tears leaked from her eyes and she laid an arm across his stomach and let them fall, wetting his naked chest."

"I...I'm sorry, Lucky. So sorry."

"Shh. Now. It's all right. We'll be all right. Just sleep."

When next she awoke, light peeked through the drapes. She reached for Lucky but he was gone and his side of the bed, cold."

Tears welled in her eyes. He'd left her,

after all.

Lucky come through the door carrying a tray.

"Here now. What's the matter?"

She breathed out a sigh of relief at hearing his voice.

"I thought you'd left me. That you'd changed your mind and decided I wasn't worth your time, that I—"

He set the tray on the bureau and went to the bed. Lucky sat down next to her.

"Ava. Don't think like that. I'm not leaving. Not now, not ever. You're my wife and whether you believe me or not, I do love you. Just because we disagree with each other doesn't change my feelings for you."

"You left last night."

"And I returned. I knew as soon as I stepped out the door that I'd made a mistake but I was so angry, I needed to calm down. I went downstairs and was preparing to go to the Golden Spike when Jack came out of his office."

"Did Jack go with you?"

"I didn't go. I talked to Jack for a while and then came back up here. You were crying in your sleep, and seeing you like that broke my heart."

His eyebrows came together and she saw the pain in his eyes.

"I shed my clothes and climbed in bed. You immediately scooted over to me and I held you in my arms. You stopped weeping."

"I miss her...or him. I feel a big hole in my body where she was."

"The pain is a hole in your heart, my love."

He placed his fist over his heart.

"The same that I feel. No longer will I see her grow within your body or feel her when she begins to move. Jack told me the things I could expect to go through. He's had other children, you see. They were murdered."

She closed her eyes and rested her head on his chest, tears falling for Jack and the pain he must have felt.

"Oh, my God. I didn't know."

Lucky shrugged.

"He doesn't talk about it, or them, very much. He's told Rita, of course, but very few others."

"Just as you told me about Tess. You wanted me to understand and I didn't." Ava's chest hurt. So much sadness. "I'm not sure I do now, not all of it, but I understand enough to know you'll not love me like you did her."

She turned her face away.

He brought her back with a single finger to her chin.

"That was then. This is now. I can't let the past color my...our...future. Nor can you. We will always have each other, but we will have other children, too. We mustn't lose sight of that fact. Trust me, Ava."

"I do trust you. And I love you. But I have to know why you said what you did to Emmett? About getting another mail-order bride."

"I didn't want him to think I cared. I was trying to keep you safe by convincing him I didn't care about you. None of what I said was true. I can never replace you."

He rubbed her uninjured arm.

She leaned back her head so she could see his face and looked into his whiskey brown eyes and saw the same sadness that she herself felt.

He is hurting like I am. How could I think he didn't care?

"How can I be sure you really do love me and this isn't just something you know I want to hear?"

He took her hand and laid it on his chest over his heart.

"Do you feel the beat there?"

"Yes."

"Every beat represents my love for you. If I can't convince you that I love you and have you love me in return, this beat will stop."

His brows lowered in a frown.

"I'll have no reason to carry on."

"Oh, Lucky." Her heart beat faster and she thought healed some knowing that he loved her, truly.

She laid her head on his chest and hugged him.

"I don't like when we fight. I'm sorry I—"

"No, don't be sorry. You have a right to your feelings, just as I have a right to mine."

CHAPTER 15

Six weeks had passed since Ava lost the baby. She was healing physically and emotionally. The doctor said they could resume relations, but she hadn't told Lucky. She wasn't ready.

She was in the shop putting the finishing touches on Rita's ring. She had a large magnifying glass on a stand and held the ring under it. With a very fine grained file she filed off the extra gold from the mold. When she was done with that she shined the ring and then set the diamond. She should have it finished by tomorrow.

She was making the last filing touches when Lucky came in.

Ava looked up at him and smiled.

"Hi. Stop by to take your wife to lunch?"

"No. I ran into Doctor Goad."

His eyebrows lowered and he frowned.

"What did you two talk about?"

Lucky put his hands on his hips.

"Something you and I should have talked about weeks ago."

"Oh." She refocused on filing the edges of the ring. "And what is that?"

"The doctor asked me if you had suffered any pain when we resumed having relations. I told him no. We are fine."

He took a deep breath and his eyebrows relaxed.

"But we're not fine. You didn't tell me you were healed."

"I figured I'd tell you when I was ready. I'm not, so no reason to tell you."

"Ava, what's wrong? Why are you afraid for us to make love?"

She wrung her hands.

"It could happen again."

"What could happen? That you'd get pregnant or that you'd miscarry? Which is it you fear?"

"Both." She turned away and looked at the closed curtains on the window. "If I become pregnant, I could lose the babe and I don't think I can go through that again."

Lucky came up behind her, wrapped his arms around her waist and rested his chin on her shoulder.

"Have you decided you don't want any

children?"

"No. I do want kids, but I'm…I'm afraid."

There she'd said it. She'd admitted her fear.

"My love, many ways exist for us to be together and you not to conceive."

She rested her arms on his at her waist.

"How can that be?" She'd missed their connection so much, had she kept them apart longer than necessary by not discussing what the doctor told her?

"Will you trust me to make love to you and to use those methods until you are ready?"

She looked up into his face and saw him smile.

His eyes conveyed the truth. He would take care of her, protect her.

"All right. I'll trust you. Tonight you can show me how you'll keep us safe."

*****

That night Lucky made sweet love to Ava. She didn't think he'd ever been so gentle or so caring, except maybe their first time, but since then they'd both enjoyed more rousing lovemaking. But tonight was special, this was the time for him to show her she really could trust him, but even so, she was unprepared when he covered himself with something.

"What are you doing?"

"I'm protecting you. This will prevent my seed from entering you so you cannot get pregnant. When you're ready, we'll stop doing this and take our chances we can still make babies."

Alarmed, her stomach turned. "Do you think we won't be able to make more babies?"

"No. I'm sure we can but I've known some couples who are only blessed with one child. That won't be us, Ava."

His voice was strong and sure. But was she preventing them from having children at all? How did becoming pregnant all work? Was a man's seed only potent for a specific length of time? Lord, she wished she knew. Now was not a good time to learn that Jeffrey hadn't taught her everything after all. All she knew for sure was that she wanted more children and Lucky was making sure she wouldn't have any until she was ready.

What did being ready mean? Ready to be a mother? Yes, she was ready. Her heart smiled at the thought of a babe in her arms.

Was she willing to risk losing another child? No. Going through that again would kill her. All the pain, she remembered how much she hurt inside, how empty she felt.

Was she willing to risk one for the other?

Yes, she was willing to risk anything to be a mother.

She and Lucky lay cuddling after having made love. Ava smiled that she could say truthfully, they had made love not had relations.

"Lucky." She rubbed her hand on his chest, enjoying the way the soft curls of hair felt on her fingers

"Yes, sweetheart." He stroked her back as she rested against him.

"I want a baby."

He stopped his movements. "Are you sure? We've only used protection one time."

"I'm sure." She trailed a finger over his chest. "Even if we lose another one, we have to keep trying. I want children and the older I get the less likely that will happen. Don't use the protection anymore. We'll take our chances, just like everyone else. Hopefully, we'll be blessed."

"Have I ever told you how wonderful I

think you are?"

Grinning, she rested her leg across his. "No, but you can tell me now."

He laughed and pulled her up for a kiss.

"You, my dear wife, are amazing."

He kissed both her eyelids.

She laughed

"I saw that ring you made for Rita and you're talented as a jewelry designer."

He kissed her nose.

She stopped him and kissed his mouth. He opened for her and she took the lead, kissing him the way he'd taught her and with all the love in her heart.

"You're going to be a wonderful mother and you're already a great wife."

He pulled her on top of him, so she straddled his hips.

"I love you more every day."

She smiled and kissed his chin.

"And I you."

"Make love to me."

"Like this? I don't know how."

He grinned and showed her.

*****

May 1, 1870

Lucky lowered the newspaper he'd

borrowed from Jack's office.

"They are starting on the house today. Do you want to watch?"

Ava swallowed her eggs. "No. I can't imagine there will be anything to see of much interest for quite some time." *Besides I might miss out on some 'auntie' time with baby Brad.*

"Did you see the baby this morning? The little guy is getting bigger every day but he's still awfully small."

She rolled her eyes. "Of course they're small. How else would they be born?"

"We haven't seen Jack and Rita at breakfast since he was born."

Ava picked up her coffee cup. "Brad is a demanding little fellow. He keeps Mama busy." She sipped her drink.

"Daddy, too, apparently."

"I resemble that remark," said Jack as he entered the dining room for breakfast.

Lucky laughed. "I wondered if I'd see you today. Little Brad has been keeping you both hoppin'."

"Who knew that having a baby could be so tiring?" asked Jack. He prepared a plate of food and carried it to Rita's place at the table. Then he went back to the side board and filled a plate of his own.

Rita entered carrying their three-week-old baby.

Ava pushed away her plate. She was done eating anyway.

"Oh, let me see that sweet baby," said Ava.

She held up her arms for the child.

Leaning, Rita placed the baby into Ava's arms.

Rita sat next to Ava.

"I'm so glad you two are still living here. It's been a great help to have you help with Brad."

Ava smiled. Now was the perfect time to share her news. "We love to. He's such a sweet baby. I hope ours is as good natured. Isn't that right Brad? You'll show our little one how to be a good baby won't you."

"Yours?" repeated Rita.

"Ours?" asked Lucky, an eyebrow lifted.

"Ours," said Ava, grinning. "I went to see the doctor yesterday. We can expect him or her around Thanksgiving."

Lucky went to his wife and hugged her shoulders, gently.

"Are you happy with this news?" he asked.

She gazed up into his face. His brow was furrowed. "Yes, I'm thrilled. And you?"

He leaned down and kissed her.

"I can't think of anything I want more."

Rita approached where Ava sat and then gave her a hug.

"I'm so happy for you."

Jack slapped Lucky on the back.

"Congratulations."

"I hope you have a girl. We can betroth them to each other," teased Rita.

"As much as I love this little guy," said Ava. "I want them both to make their own choice of who to marry."

"Me, too," said Lucky. "I want them to be as happy as their parents are."

"That's a good point." Rita sat next to Ava at the dining table. Jack sat at the head with Lucky to his left.

"How long before they finish your house?" asked Jack.

"Tired of us being here?" asked Lucky.

"Heavens no, especially now. I don't know what we'll do when you move out."

"You'll figure it out just as we will," said Lucky with a jut of his chin toward Ava and the baby. "More than likely we'll see just as much of each other as we do now."

Ava passed the baby back to Rita and stood.

"If you'll excuse us, I have some things to talk to my husband about."

Jack laughed.

"For some reason, I bet very little talking will get done."

Ava shook her head and smiled, then held out her hand for Lucky.

They walked out of the dining room and then when they were in the hall and no one would see, they broke into a run. When they arrived at their room both were out of breath.

She stood next to the bed, facing him. "I hope you don't mind that I broke the news the way I did. I just couldn't wait any longer to tell you."

"I don't mind. We would have told Jack and Rita immediately anyway."

She felt giddy as a school girl, almost as if this was their first time together. She unbuttoned her blouse and then unbuttoned her skirt and let them both fall in a heap on the floor.

Lucky followed suit with his own clothes.

In minutes, both were naked and holding

each other on the bed.

Lucky kissed her, his tongue pressing for entrance that was gladly given. His hand caressed her leg and then was on her stomach.

He broke the kiss and looked down at her belly.

"Do you see it? See the bump where our baby lay growing?"

"I do."

He flattened his hand onto her stomach.

"I can't wait until he begins to move and kick. Until I feel him under my hand when I touch your stomach. Until you're big as a house, carrying my baby."

"Big as a house? That's what you want to see?"

"Yes. That's what I want because, you see, I love you, all of you and when you're heavy with my babe, I'll love you as much then as I do now."

"Oh," she furrowed her brow and caressed his jaw. "You do know how to make my heart beat faster."

"I love you, Ava, or Jane, or whatever name you choose to be. I'll always love you."

"And I love you. I guess you're *lucky* in

love after all." She giggled at her joke.

He silenced her laughter with his lips, kissing her each time she started to say anything more.

Finally, she simply wrapped her arms around her husband and kissed him back.

EPILOGUE

November 20, 1870
The card room in the Madigan home.

Lucky prowled like a cat, back and forth across the carpet.

"How can you be so calm? What if something goes wrong? Ava's just a little thing…"

"Lucky, sit down and play your hand." Jack nodded toward the cards on the table. "There's not a thing you can do to help Ava. The baby will come when it's time. Rita and Mrs. Bates are there to help the doctor. She's in the best of hands."

"You're right. I know you're right, but I can't help but want to be there to make sure Ava is okay. And you were the same way with Rita. We were playing cards the night Brad was born as well."

"You'd only get in the way." Jack threw his cards on the table. "Fathers are not supposed to be there when their children are

CYNTHIA WOOLF

born. I'm out. My hands lousy."

"I wish it was different. I want to make sure that Ava is doing fine."

"Of course, she is. The baby probably hasn't even started coming yet. Not one sound of yelling from upstairs."

"Rita didn't holler when Brad was born," said Lucky, standing and staring at the ceiling.

"And I didn't play cards any better than you are. It's a good thing we aren't playing for money."

"What?"

Lucky looked at Jack.

"What are we playing for?"

"Naming rights."

Lucky's eyes widened. "You can't be serious."

Jack laughed.

"Of course, I'm not serious. Now come—"

Whatever Jack would have said was cut off by the cry of a baby.

Lucky threw his cards on the table and ran upstairs to his and Ava's bedroom.

He stopped at the open door, both hands on the door frame bracing him. He looked over at Ava searching her face for evidence of pain.

"Did I hear a baby?"

Another cry sounded and Lucky looked toward the source of the noise. Dr. Goad was holding a baby upside down by its feet. Since he could only see the back, he didn't know what gender of child he had.

Then he heard another cry. This time the sound came from over by Ava.

"What the…?"

Ava laughed.

"Come here and meet your daughter."

He walked over to his wife, kissed her on the lips and then looked down at the bundle in her lap.

She unwrapped the child, her moves slow and careful.

He saw he had a daughter with ten toes and ten fingers and a loud voice for a new born. What hair she had was brown and there wasn't a lot of it.

The baby squirmed and fussed starting to cry.

"She's unhappy at being naked in the cold room," said Ava. She wrapped up the baby and laid the child on the bed beside her.

"Here comes your son," said Mrs. Bates.

She carried the little bundle and gave him to Lucky.

Lucky looked down on his son. This baby had a head full of pale blond hair.

"He's so small. They are both so small." He couldn't keep the wonder out of his voice.

"How did we have two? Did you know we were having two?"

Ava looked over at the doctor and smiled.

"The doctor and I weren't sure until six weeks ago. And then I didn't want to tell you, just in case something happened. Are you happy with your surprise?"

He looked at his children, his heart pounding. "I'm thrilled. Now we can use both names that we chose. Vivian Leigh Madigan and Jeffrey James Madigan."

"Jeffrey would be so pleased to know that his nephew is named after him."

Tears rolled down Ava's cheeks.

"I know you miss him. I'm glad we're naming our son after your brother."

Lucky looked around and discovered he and Ava were quite alone with their babies. Rita, Mrs. Bates and the doctor had all left the little family to get acquainted.

"Twins are always smaller than average. The doctor said Vivian weighs five pounds two ounces and Jeffrey is a bounder at five and a half pounds."

"So tiny." Jeffrey's length was barely the distance between Lucky's hand to his elbow.

"They'll grow quickly."

Vivian wailed and, as soon as he heard his sister cry, so did Jeffrey.

"They are hungry. I can feed them both at the same time, if I hold them with their feet on my ribs. I'll get Vivian settled and then you can help me with Jeffrey. In the mean time try and calm him."

"I don't know how."

"Talk to him. Let him know you're his father."

Lucky sat on the bed next to Ava. He held the baby close and talked softly

"Hi there, son."

The baby quieted and looked toward the sound.

Lucky held the baby in the crook of his arm. "I'm your daddy and Mama and I love you dearly. You and Vivian are loved and wanted so very much. Do you know that? Yes, you are."

He looked from the baby to Ava. "He has your eyes. They're violet."

"Oh, good. They both have them, then. Just like my twin, my Jeffrey and me."

He kissed the baby's forehead and then his cheeks. His heart was so full of love it nearly burst forth from his chest.

"I love you, son."

Lucky looked over at Ava as she nursed Vivian.

"I love you, too, little Vivian."

"Do you think they have any idea of how much we love them?"

Ava gazed up at him.

"Not yet, but we'll make sure they do."

ABOUT THE AUTHOR

Cynthia Woolf is the award winning and best-selling author of twenty-seven historical western romance books and two short stories with more books on the way.

Cynthia loves writing and reading romance. Her first western romance Tame A Wild Heart, was inspired by the story her mother told her of meeting Cynthia's father on a ranch in Creede, Colorado. Although Tame A Wild Heart takes place in Creede that is the only similarity between the stories. Her father was a cowboy not a bounty hunter and her mother was a nursemaid (called a nanny now) not the ranch owner. The ranch they met on is still there as part of the open space in Mineral County in southwestern Colorado.

Writing as CA Woolf she has six scifi, space opera romance titles. She calls them westerns in space.

Cynthia credits her wonderfully supportive husband Jim and her great critique partners for saving her sanity and allowing her to explore her creativity.

TITLES AVAILABLE

THE DANCING BRIDE, Central City Brides, Book 1
THE SAPPHIRE BRIDE, Central City Brides, Book 2

GENEVIEVE: Bride of Nevada, American Mail-Order
Brides Series

THE HUNTER BRIDE – Hope's Crossing, Book 1
THE REPLACEMENT BRIDE – Hope's Crossing,
Book 2
THE STOLEN BRIDE – Hope's Crossing, Book 3
THE UNEXPECTED BRIDE – Hope's Crossing,
Book 4

GIDEON – The Surprise Brides

MAIL ORDER OUTLAW – The Brides of Tombstone,
Book 1
MAIL ORDER DOCTOR – The Brides of Tombstone,
Book 2
MAIL ORDER BARON – The Brides of Tombstone,
Book 3

NELLIE – The Brides of San Francisco 1
ANNIE – The Brides of San Francisco 2
CORA – The Brides of San Francisco 3
SOPHIA – The Brides of San Francisco 4
AMELIA – The Brides of San Francisco 5

JAKE (Book 1, Destiny in Deadwood series)
LIAM (Book 2, Destiny in Deadwood series)
ZACH (Book 3, Destiny in Deadwood series)

CAPITAL BRIDE (Book 1, Matchmaker & Co. series)
HEIRESS BRIDE (Book 2, Matchmaker & Co. series)

FIERY BRIDE (Book 3, Matchmaker & Co. series)
COLORADO BRIDE (Book 4, Matchmaker & Co. series)

TAME A WILD HEART (Book 1, Tame series)
TAME A WILD WIND (Book 2, Tame series)
TAME A WILD BRIDE (Book 3, Tame series)
TAME A HONEYMOON HEART (novella, Tame series)

THORPE'S MAIL-ORDER BRIDE, Montana Sky Series (Kindle Worlds)
KISSED BY A STRANGER, Montana Sky Series (Kindle Worlds)
A FAMILY FOR CHRISTMAS, Montana Sky Series (Kindle Worlds)

WEBSITE – http://cynthiawoolf.com/

NEWSLETTER - http://bit.ly/1qBWhFQ

Made in the USA
Coppell, TX
01 November 2023

23705862R00154